My Always ONE

ALEATHA ROMIG
NEW YORK TIMES BESTSELLING AUTHOR

A friends-to-lovers 'lighter' stand-alone

ALEATHA ROMIG

New York Times, Wall Street Journal, and USA Today
bestselling author of the Devil's Series, Sparrow Webs,
Infidelity series, Consequences series, and Lighter Ones

AUTHOR'S *Note*

Over five years ago, my friend Georgia Cates and I decided to start an adventure: writing stories that were outside of our brand. Our endeavor was successful on many counts. It opened a world of possibilities and let us shake off the chains of expectation. Though we each wrote different titles, we ventured into that new world under one name.

While that pen name no longer exists, it helped us expand our horizons, allowing us to try new things.

The story you're about to read started as a short, sexy, and predictable novella written by me as Jade Sinner and entitled ASHTON – THE AGREEMENT. My reviews were good, and I learned that while writing dark twists and turns, I could also be sexy, funny, and light.

If any part of this story seems familiar, it could be because you read the 19K-word novella a while ago. Those stories are no longer available.

MY ALWAYS ONE is much more!

It is now a stand-alone, full-length contemporary-romance novel.

I hope this story makes you swoon, laugh, and finish the last page with a smile.

I know that I did all of those things while writing it.

Thank you for allowing me to shed the other name and embrace this side of Aleatha. Thank you for giving the lighter side of Aleatha a chance.

I hope you enjoy MY ALWAYS ONE!

ALEATHA ROMIG
NEW YORK TIMES BESTSELLING AUTHOR

A friends-to-lovers 'lighter' stand-alone

When we were young, Samantha Anderson was the girl down the street. For as long as I remember, she's been my partner in crime, in adventures, and in almost everything. Sami is fun and sexy, my greatest confidant, and my best friend.

From early on, we vow that our relationship will never change—through thick and thin, we'll remain always and forever in the friend zone. We will not cross *that* line.

After all, I'm not a forever kind of guy.

Then *that* line blurs.

We amend our agreement.

Best friends become friends with benefits.
   Is this new agreement the key to our future? Or will I lose my best friend?

MY ALWAYS ONE is a new, fun, and sexy friends-to-lovers contemporary romance. A

steamy stand-alone, MY ALWAYS ONE is not connected to any other of Aleatha's Lighter Ones and may be read on its own.

CHAPTER
One

Marshal
Ten Years Ago

"You're such an ass," Sami blurts out, shaking her head. Her tone sounds angry, but her volume is still low.

I shrug with a smirk as I heave my backpack higher on my shoulder. As we step through the front doors of our high school, I squint my eyes at the onslaught of the warm Michigan sunshine. For a few steps I think about how to answer her, what to say. If Sami were a guy, I'd have the perfect response. I'd say that I wasn't the ass, but Maura Sharpe had a fine one.

The thing is that Sami isn't a guy; she's my best friend. I know that fact without a doubt. I also know she isn't interested in my thoughts regarding Maura's nice round...

Even thinking of telling her, I imagine Sami scrunching her cute little nose and after hitting me, half-heartedly saying, *Disgusting, TMI.*

Trying to avoid her manhandling—something I wouldn't take from anyone else—I start to reply when Sami purposely bumps her shoulder against mine. "I thought we had an understanding." Her tiny frame nearly bounces me from the sidewalk.

I grin her direction as I walk the balance beam of the curb.

So much for my attempt to avoid her physical aggression.

Steadying my place on the sidewalk, I narrowly miss falling to the pavement and being picked off as a car peels past, no doubt determined to leave the high school parking lot before the line backs up at the stoplight. Flashing my brightest smile, I avoid Sami's comment and stare down at her and with a gleam in my eyes ask, "Are you trying kill me?"

Sami shakes her head in reply and continues her interrogation. "Maura? Maura?"

Each time she asks, repeating the name belonging to her friend and my latest conquest, her voice gets louder and the name more exaggerated. I avoid answering as we weave through the parking lot until I hit the unlock button on my key fob. With a huff, Sami goes around to the passenger side of my old truck.

Once we're both inside, I start the engine and immediately roll down the windows. Michigan weather needs therapy. I swear it has serious multiple-personality issues

—freezing one day and then sweltering the next. It's as if the weather has as much trouble deciding what it wants as I do.

Sami lifts her long brown hair from her neck and directs the air conditioning vent toward her before glaring my direction.

"What do you want me to say?" I finally ask as I put the truck in reverse and begin backing out of the space, barely missing two girls walking with their heads together, too lost in their conversation to realize they're about to become roadkill.

As my brakes squeal, one of the girls turns and glares my direction, but as soon as she recognizes my truck, her anger morphs to a smile. Her head tilts and her eyes search for mine in the side mirror.

"Hi, Marshal," she calls with the telltale flick of her neck and a finger wave. "Call me."

I wave at the same time I see Sami's head shake in my peripheral vision. As I ease the truck out of the parking space, I say a silent prayer that the girl in the mirror won't try to come up to my open window.

Sami cranes her neck over her shoulder. "Isn't she a freshman?"

"Is she? I think that means she'll soon be a sophomore."

"Jeez, Marshal. You really are a manwhore. You know that?"

I lift my brows. "No, Sami, I'm not a whore. Those who practice one of the oldest professions do so to be paid. No one pays me. I willingly share my talents with those in need. I think that's called being a humanitarian. Consider it as my service to women everywhere. Maybe I should add that to my college application under the title of community service."

Sami shakes her head. "You've already been accepted to Michigan State without that bit of information." She takes in a deep breath. "You know, if I hadn't known you since we were five, I don't think I'd like you."

"But you have and you do," I say with a grin.

"I just..."

I finally maneuver the truck out of the parking lot and onto the side streets. Hitting the gas, I pick up speed and bring a nice breeze through the open windows, helping to cool the cab. Admittedly, the acceleration works better than my AC.

One day, I won't be driving a beat-up old truck. One day, I'll have a car that fits with my body and personality.

"Maura's my friend," Sami says.

"Maura's a big girl. She knew what she was doing. Actually, she knew—"

Sami lifts her hand. "Stop. You know our deal. No details. I don't want to know about the little freshman or Maura or anyone else."

"Well, let me just say that if we're doing a comparison study, Maura is much more experienced than the freshman, but in the grand scheme, she can learn a bit too."

"Noted. But you know that Maura just broke up with Matt." Sami shakes her head. "And right before prom. Seriously, Marsh, the last thing she needs is you using her for a one-night stand."

I reach over and squeeze Sami's leg. "You know me. I don't use girls. They come to me."

"Because you're so freaking fantastic in the sack?"

My cheek rises, creating my cocky, lopsided signature grin. "That *is* the word on the street."

"Word on the street is Matt's going to kick your ass."

I can't help but scoff. "Right. I'd love to see him try. Besides, I got the whole story. Maura broke up with him because she found out he was doing Laura."

Sami turns with her mouth agape. "Laura? Cheerleader Laura? Debate team Laura?"

I nod.

"Maura told me he cheated, but not with who."

"I guess girls are just willing to share anything to elicit my sympathy favors."

She sighs and lays her head against the seat. "Is that all you want out of life?"

I look over at my best friend. There's something about Sami that makes her different than every other girl I've ever known. Maybe it's that we've known each other since we were kids, or that we know everything about one another, or maybe that we swore never to lie to one another, and we haven't. I'm not sure of the reason, but for the first time since I was balls deep in Maura Sharpe, I feel a little bad about it.

Which is strange.

I never feel regret.

Euphoria, an amazing, fantastic release, yes, but never regret.

"Sami, what is it?"

She turns toward the open window, her hair blowing in the breeze, and takes a minute before she answers. "I think it's that we're graduating in a few weeks. Things are changing. Look at us. We're going off to two different colleges, and we have friends getting married."

"We also have friends with kids on the way. Do you want that to be you?"

Sami looks at me for a minute and then turns back to the open window. "Someday."

"Someday, but not now. Not at eighteen."

After another sigh, she leans back against the seat. In the few seconds that passed, her fun smile, the one that has gotten us both in trouble more times than I can count, is back. "Then, Mr. Michaels, keep your cock in your pants."

"Don't worry. I have a lifetime supply of wraps. I'm well practiced at safe sex."

"That's good to know, but some people think of it as more than sex."

"Define it," I say with a knowing grin. When she doesn't answer, I do. "It is sex, Sami. No strings. It's my way of life."

"Do you think about the girl?"

"Of course. I'm not a monster. I also don't give off any false vibes of commitment."

"Well, for your information, Maura has been texting me all day. She's sure she's *in love*. She knows you're going stag to the prom and has a plan that includes forever." I start to talk, but Sami is on a roll. "And by the way, according to her, *you're the best*." Her voice does this sing-song thing when she relays Maura's messages.

"Oh, I am *the best*, but *love* and *forever*? No way." I shake my head. "I told her the same thing I tell them all: I'm not a commitment kind of guy."

"She mentioned that," Sami says. "She also asked me about your favorite color. Your favorite food. Your favorite TV show...on and on. She's got it bad."

I bypass the street to our neighborhood and keep driving.

As familiar scenes pass by the truck windows, I chastise myself.

I knew better than to do it with Sami's friend...that was our understanding. Sami's connection makes it harder to walk away. The thing is that I didn't find Maura or go looking for her.

She found me.

I should have followed my gut and told Maura no.

In my defense, I did—the first time and second. A man can only say no so many times. And Maura was persistent. She also spoke not only to my good sense but to another part of my anatomy—the part that has a mind of its own.

"Where are we going?" Sami asks as she looks out at the freshly cultivated fields.

"How about coffee? We can go to the shop in Spencer and avoid *friends*." Yes, I mean Maura.

Sami shakes her head. "No, I'm broke."

"I'll buy," I offer, but we both know I don't have much money either.

"No. How about the lake?" She smiles up at the blue sky. "It's too nice to be inside."

I nod, seeing the blue sky and sunshine.

A few minutes and a few dirt roads later, we're beyond the Johnson city limits. I pull down a well-traveled lane and we come to a stop. Parking, I turn off my truck. The lake Sami mentioned isn't big. It isn't one surrounded by homes or summer cottages. The best part of it is that it's kind of isolated. The entire lake is located on private property owned by some guy who lives far away. By the look of the old gate permanently removed from its hinges, he hasn't been here in years, maybe decades.

Over time, the lake has become one of the hangouts for local teenagers. It's not just used by teenagers though. Dads bring their kids here to fish all year round. Because of its size, it freezes to a safe thickness for ice fishing, and in the warmer weather they wade into the water or stand on the shore. In the heat of the summer, families who don't have their own cottages or lake access come here to swim.

We won't be swimming. Not today.

This is only mid-May and it's too early in the year. The water would be freezing cold.

I lead as we walk through the tall grass to the edge of the lake and up an embankment to some high rocks. It's the perfect spot. From this height you can see down into the depths of the dark water and over to the lane. No one can sneak up on you here, and you can see on forever. It's like being on the top of the world.

"Truth or dare," I say once we both settle on the warm rock.

Sami sways her shoulders back and forth as she contemplates my question. "Truth. You know I'd never lie to you."

"Are you still holding out?"

She smiles with her eyes gazing down. "Do you mean have I put out yet?"

"I mean, has Todd gotten in your pants yet?"

"Those are two different questions. Pick one."

My neck straightens and my chest aches a little at the thought of that dickhead with his hands down Sami's shorts. After all, I'm a guy, and I know how guys can be. I don't like the idea of anyone doing that to her.

I guess I feel protective of her.

Then I remind myself that Sami is my friend. What she does is her business, not mine. I have no right to expect her to stay a virgin when I'm screwing every other girl out there. "First one," I say, asking if she's still a virgin.

"I still am, but I don't think it can last much longer."

I sit taller. "Sami, if that ass is pressuring you..."

"That's not what I mean. I mean, I think I want to. You yourself boasted of Maura's expertise. It makes me think that I'm the last one out there, a unicorn."

"Aren't unicorns a good thing?" I smile at my memories. "I remember this freckled little girl who had unicorn wallpaper in her bedroom."

"For the record, you know I hated that wallpaper."

"Don't do prom night, Sami. It's too cliché."

"That's what Maura said."

Oh great.

Sami went on, "I just don't know if Todd's the forever kind of guy. I want forever, but I also want..." She grins. "College and adventure." She leans back on her arms and looks up at the crystal blue sky. "I don't know what I want."

"We don't have to decide right now, do we?"

"Now, it's your turn," she says.

Sitting up and leaning near the edge, I peer down at the water. The lake is easily twenty feet below us. In the summer there were many times we'd jumped from this very spot into the cool spring-fed lake below. "Give it your best shot."

"Okay. Truth or dare?"

I look up at her sparkling green eyes and realize that she's thinking the same thing—the water. I can practically see her consider getting up and jumping or making me jump. She would do it too, clothes and all. It's part of what I love about her.

It's not that I don't want to jump. If it were summer and twenty degrees warmer, I wouldn't hesitate, but well, my better sense replies, "Truth."

Her lips come together for a moment before she smiles. "Do you think you'll ever be a forever kind of guy?"

Shit! That isn't what I expected.

I sigh as I lay back on the warm rock and stretch out my legs. "Truth?"

"Always."

"I really don't see forever in my future. I'm selfish and I know that. I don't have any desire to change. I don't see me being committed to anyone but myself. I know that makes me sound like an ass, and I probably am, but forever is a really long time."

Sami lays her head back beside me. "What if I never find that forever guy?"

I reach over and squeeze her hand. "You will, but if you don't, you'll always have me."

"Always?"

"Always and forever."

CHAPTER
Two

Sami
Eight years ago

I practically bounce on my toes when I see Marshal's truck turn down the street. I can't believe he came all the way to Ann Arbor for me. In reality, I didn't ask him to do it. I just texted him and told him how upset I was that Josh had to leave town for a job interview.

Josh and I have been dating since the beginning of my freshman year. Now, I'm finishing my sophomore year, and Josh is about to graduate with a degree in kinesiology. I've never seen him as excited as he is about the job possibility. It's in Detroit, working for the Lions' organization. Josh recently completed his internship with the U of M football team, and working with the professionals is his dream.

My sorority has its big end-of-the-year dance tomorrow night. In many ways it's like prom on a fancier and more intimate level.

I've been excited about the dance for weeks. Since

freshmen can't attend, this is my first one. Josh was looking forward to it too until he received the call. He's a finalist for the position he wants, and they want him and the other applicant to spend the weekend in multiple interviews as well as social engagements, getting to know members of the staff and the owners.

Of course, I encouraged him to go. I'd even told him, "This is just a dance. There'll be another one next year."

Yes, I am thinking forever.

Marshal's truck pulls into the space in front of my friend Rita's apartment as I run to the sidewalk and wait for him to open the door. A smile fills my face as I see my best friend. From his light brown hair to his cocky grin, it's hard to imagine him as the scrawny little boy who moved in down the block.

Even though he's not playing football at Michigan State, Marshal has grown into a man, tall, solid, and muscular. Sometimes when I see him, I think of him like a brother. The truth is that Marsh and I are closer than I am with my brother. Byron—my brother—is a good guy, but being he's three years older, we aren't close, not like Marshal and I.

And then sometimes, like now, as he opens the door of his truck and flashes me a *Marshal special smile,* I see him the way other girls do—for the incredibly handsome man he's become.

It's no wonder girls throw themselves at him.

"I can't believe you came all this way," I say as I run toward him and wrap my arms around his neck.

Marshal laughs as he twirls me around and sets my feet back on the ground. "Are you kidding? What's a six-hour drive to see my best friend?"

He reaches inside his truck and pulls out a long hanging bag.

"You really have a suit?"

"Of course I do." He flings the bag over his shoulder. "I could make it a full-time job going to sorority dances."

"Am I keeping you from one of your groupies?"

He reaches around me and tugs me close. "Well, there are probably tears in Lansing." He grins. "No, I'm right where I want to be. I wouldn't miss being your stand-in for anything or anyone."

I briefly lay my head on his shoulder. "I've missed you." Pulling away, I reach for his hand. "Come with me. Rita's roommate moved out, and she's letting us stay here this weekend."

"I thought you'd sneak me into the sorority house," he says as he wiggles his eyebrows.

I fake a gasp. "Don't tell me that you've been snuck into sorority houses up at Michigan State? It's against the rules."

"Um, of course not." He laughs. "Since when did you become a rule follower?"

I lead him into the building and down the corridor to Rita's apartment. "Oh, I know you, Marshal Michaels. If

I snuck you into my sorority house, it would be like taking a five-year-old you to a candy store and saying, take your pick."

We step inside.

It's a nice apartment for college students with a simple floor plan: living room, kitchen, one bathroom, and two bedrooms. The glass doors in the living room are open to the patio, letting the spring breeze flutter the lightweight curtains.

Marshal lays his hanging bag and duffel bag on the couch and says, "It's a good thing we're not there if I'm only supposed to choose one."

I shake my head. "Some things never change."

"They don't. I couldn't let my best friend miss her big end-of-the-year dance."

"I hope it will be better than prom."

"I told you not to do it."

I roll my eyes. "Oh, wise one, one day I'll listen to you."

"Where's Rita?" he asks.

"She's staying with a friend and said we could have her apartment for the weekend."

"A friend?" His eyebrows dance.

I scrunch my nose. "Do you remember when you were here last time and met a guy named Marvin?"

"You'd think I'd remember that name."

"He was at that party we went to off campus."

Marshal's brow furrows. "Tall guy, talked about

himself all the time? His dad owns some big construc-
tion company?"

"Agricultural co-ops, but yeah, that's him. Well, he
and Rita have been dating for a few months and..."

He lifted his hand. "Stop. I can fill in the blanks."

"I bet you can."

This obviously isn't Marshal's first visit to my
campus, and I've been up to his on multiple occasions.
He was right, six hours isn't too long to visit your best
friend. With all of our visits, this is the first rescue
mission, and I can't let it pass without thanking him. "I
mean it, Marsh, thank you."

He reaches for me, laying his palm on my cheek. "I'll
never let you down."

My face inclines to his touch.

"Am I supposed to get you a corsage or something?"

I shake my head. "No, and remember, I'm allergic to
roses."

"No, you're not. You just don't like them since that
kid in middle school sent you a bouquet."

"His name was Lee and who sends roses at thirteen?"

Marshal smiled. "Hey, if I'm not getting my pick of
your sorority sisters, tell me that you plan to feed me
well."

That's my Marshal. He's smart as can be, but his two
favorite subjects are girls and food.

It's a big weekend on campus, the last before finals,
and the mood is joyous everywhere we go. We both have

friends who go to both of our schools. After pizza at one of the local hangouts, Marshal gets a text from Jordon, a guy who graduated two years before us from our high school.

Marshal looks up from his phone. "Jordon invited us to Delta Tau Delta. He said they're having a blow-out party."

I can't help but sigh. "They're always having big parties."

Marshal sits back against his chair and narrows his gaze. "Why don't you want to go?"

"Todd will be there."

"Oh yeah, Mr. Thirty Seconds."

"Shut up." Sometimes I wish I wasn't so honest with Marshal, but as his lopsided grin grows, I can't help but smile too. "Fine," I say with a shake of my head.

"This is your weekend, Sami. We'll do whatever you want."

"Josh won't be thrilled about me going to a party at the Delta Tau Delta house." I shrug. "Unless I can tell him you were there, not disappearing with some freshman."

"Give me more credit."

"Okay, a senior."

Marshal nods. "No, Sami, you've got me stuck like glue." He leans forward. "What did Joshy Boy say about me coming this weekend." He wiggles his eyebrows. "About the two of us alone at Rita's?"

"Josh knows how much I want to go to the dance and he knows you." I motion between us. "He knows about us and that means he's good with it."

"Is he your forever?"

I shrug. "I'm not sure." A smile comes to my lips. "He's lasted longer than Todd."

"God, I hope so."

"No," I say too loud, my cheeks warming by the second. "Dating, not sex."

"He doesn't last longer than thirty seconds?"

"Stop, that's not what I'm talking about."

At nearly ten p.m., Marshal pulls his truck into a parking spot on the street and leans my way. "Do you want me to tell Todd you've found someone better than Speedy Gonzales?"

"I'd rather not talk to Todd at all."

Marshal reaches for my hand. "Deal."

* * *

Saturday night, I step from Rita's bedroom, smoothing my dress. It's red and short and fits in all the right places. The shoes I'm wearing aren't mine. I found them in Rita's closet, and after a quick text to my friend, she said I could wear them. They're tall and slender. I figure since Marshal is taller than Josh, why not wear tall heels?

"Oh hell to the no."

I look up at my best friend.

He's freshly shaved. The sparse beard he was sporting when he arrived is gone, showing off his chiseled jawline. His light brown hair is combed back, and as my gaze lowers, I see his suit fits him like a glove. I haven't seen Marshal dressed up since our high school graduation, and I have to admit, he's changed. I mean that in a good way.

"Hey, your tie is red."

He shakes his head. "Nope. This" —he motions up and down at me— "is not going out of this apartment."

Looking down at myself and back up, I laugh as I step closer to him and grab his hand. "I love your big brother side...now shut up and be a best friend."

"First, you know Byron wouldn't let you out that door wearing that, and as for best friends, best friends don't let best friends go out into the world looking hotter than a six-alarm fire."

"Do fires have that many alarms?"

"Fuck, Sami."

"You look hot too, Marshal. We'll wow them together."

"If any other guy so much as gets close to you..."

I can't suppress my smile. "I think I know why Josh was good with you as my date." My phone rings from a distance, on the charger in the kitchen. As I go to answer it, Marshal reaches for my hand. I stop and look up at him.

"You look good, Sami."

"Thanks, so do you."

The screen says *Josh*.

I hit the green icon. "Hi."

"I'm sorry I'm not there."

"Don't worry about it. How is the weekend going?"

"Good, I think."

"What about the other candidate?"

"First, damn, Sam. That picture. You're gorgeous."

My eyes sparkle as I look at Marshal. "Don't tell me I look too good to go out. I've already heard that."

"You have?" He laughs. "Is Marshal there?"

"Yeah." I grin. "I'm looking at him right now."

"Hand him the phone."

"Um, okay." I hand the phone toward Marshal. "He wants to talk to you."

Marshal shrugs and takes the phone. I can only hear one side of the conversation, but by the way my best friend is smiling, I know it's going well. Finally, he hands it back.

"What did he say?" I ask as I cover the microphone.

"He said to lock the door and keep you inside."

My lips purse. "Seriously?"

"He said to take care of you."

"I can take care of myself."

Marshal laughed. "He said you'd say that."

"What did you tell him?"

"I said for always and forever."

I let out a breath and spoke to the phone. "Hey, for the record, I don't need men conspiring against me."

"No one is conspiring," Josh said. "We're watching over a person we love."

Love?

I felt my insides melt like a candle left too long in the sun. "Come back soon." It was all I could say.

As I hung up, I looked at Marshal. "He might be."

"Your forever?"

I nodded.

"I'm not sure I one hundred percent approve, but he seems like a good guy."

I reach for my purse and slide my phone inside. "Let's go."

CHAPTER
Three

Sami
Seven years ago

I wake as I almost fall from the twin-size mattress. This thing would be too small for me alone, but it's definitely too small for two. The musty scent of this house, shared by four college students, combines with body odor—a mixture of perspiration and too much alcohol.

I'm not a virgin, but I'm also not accustomed to waking next to a guy, especially this guy, my best friend.

When Marshal asked me to come to Michigan State for a weekend visit, I wasn't prepared for his new living conditions—four guys lacking cleaning skills or the desire to clean—or a sleepover in the same bed. I'm not sure it was all planned on his part either.

The off-campus house was rocking last night.

Marshal and his roommates may not care about cleaning, but when it comes to throwing a party, they are professionals. From the Christmas lights strung all around the backyard, to the keg, bonfire, and loud music, I'm kind of surprised no police showed up.

My stomach twists with that morning-after sensation of having too much alcohol and not enough food. I move my tongue around to try to conjure a bit of saliva.

Eww.

How can nothing taste so awful?

Then again, I'm not interested in food either. Even the thought of eating covers my skin in a new layer of perspiration.

Holding on to the edge of the small bed, I force open my eyes. The small closet-like room around us comes into focus as a rock band plays a drum solo behind my temples. Maybe if I close my eyes, I could go back to sleep. My stomach and this small bed aren't my only issues. My bladder is screaming for relief, and I seem to recall some loud voices and an order from Marshal to wake him before I leave the room.

Holding on for dear life, I nudge him as I fight for a sliver of the bed. "Marsh."

I'd considered sleeping on the floor, but decided for the sake of my health and welfare the bed was cleaner. Looking down at the carpeting, I wonder if it's only covered with dirt and stains or if there are bugs too. Again, I hang onto the edge.

"Marsh," I try again, this time adding an elbow to his back.

"What?" he says, rolling toward me.

"Whoa," I say too loudly as I throw back the sheet and spring from the bed. My bare feet squish on the carpet and my nose scrunches. "Marshal."

With only the sunlight sneaking through the mangled blinds, I see the outline of what just stabbed me and propelled me from the bed. Holy shit, my friend is equipped. I mean, he's boasted of his prowess since we were freshmen in high school, but I've never seen or thought about...

My eyes open and I know I'm staring. "Um."

I'm thinking about it now. After all, Marshal just prodded my lower back with what appears to be an erect huge dick. Taking my eyes away from my best friend's equipment tenting his shorts, I look down at the carpet and step to a dry spot, wiping my feet.

The tipped-over Solo cup eases my mind, giving me a clue of what made the carpet wet.

Stale beer is definitely better than other possibilities.

My bladder reminds me of the first reason why I woke. I reach over and shake Marshal's shoulder.

"Marshal, wake up."

Marshal's eyes open. "Sami?"

"Um" —I point to his erection— "do something with *that*. I need to use the bathroom."

"Oh. Fuck," he mumbles as he scrambles from the bed. He's high-stepping too as he lands in the moist carpet. "Shit," he says as he looks for a safe place to stand.

Once he's up—as in standing, since *up* isn't his problem—he turns away. I'm many things, but naïve isn't one of them. I have been with other guys, have a brother, and a male best friend. I can tell he's adjusting himself. "Sami, shit."

When Marshal finally turns, his cocky grin, the one he knows will save his ass and has on multiple occasions, is beaming at me. "It's morning."

I shake my head.

Finding my phone, I peer down at the screen. "It's officially afternoon." My hand goes to my head. "And I feel like shit."

"Come on," he says, "I'll go out with you and see who's up."

Even though it's nearly one in the afternoon, the

second floor is dark and quiet. All the doors are closed. When we reach the bathroom, its door is also closed. Marshal tries the doorknob. "Locked."

I wiggle on my toes, the pressure building.

Marshal reaches for my hand. "Come downstairs."

There are more signs of life on the first level. Bodies are draped over the sofa and chairs. There are even a few sleeping people on the floor. Either they're braver than I am, or they were too drunk to care when they finally fell asleep.

Around the corner, there's a small half bath under the stairs. Miraculously, the door is ajar.

"Hurry," he says, "I need to pee, too."

I scrunch my nose as I step inside. "Gross," I mumble under my breath.

Thirty minutes later, the two of us are sitting on one of the picnic tables outside McDonald's. I've downed two bottles of water and a red Gatorade, and my headache has lessened but is still present. The rock band has been exchanged for a softer jazz drummer, but apparently, the concert isn't over.

Taking a bite of my breakfast sandwich, I groan. "Jeez, I feel awful." I lift my large coffee in a mock toast. "Thanks for a great time."

Marshal grins. "You had a great time."

"Not waking to that." I tilt my chin down to what's under the table.

"I'm a guy. What do you want me to say?"

"Tell me why we had a slumber party again and why we couldn't at least go to your room. You have a normal-size bed."

"My room was already occupied."

"Eww, gross. You let other people" —I lowered my voice to a whisper— "screw in your bed?"

Marshal shrugs. "It's not a matter of letting. And I know who was in there. Bailey asked if he could use my room." He shrugs again, taking a long drink of his black coffee. "What can I say? I'm a humanitarian."

"Do you even know all those people still passed out?"

"Most of them."

I force myself to take another bite. It's a weird mind-over-matter thing. My mind knows that eating will help. My stomach isn't convinced.

The sun escapes a cloud and I notice a discolored spot on Marshal's cheek. Without thinking, I lift my hand to the spot. "Did you get hit?" Memories come back. "Wait, you got in a fight."

"Not really a fight. I told that fucker to leave."

Fucker?

"Leon?" I say and ask at the same time.

Marshal shrugs.

I remember the guy he's talking about now. Whenever I turned last night at the party, I saw him looking my direction. Eventually, he found a seat by me at the bonfire. He was one of those guys who gives off a vibe, one that says he is confident and cocky, but his said more.

It gave me a warning.

By the end of the night, he wasn't taking no for an answer.

Marshal intervened.

I drop my head to my arms on the table. "Jeez, Marsh, I'm sorry."

"Don't be."

I peek up at him from my arms. "What about Wendy? You two seemed...interested."

"Wendy will be around another night or she won't. My friend, you were more important."

"I was handling myself. I'm a big girl, you know."

Marshal lays his hand on the table. "I know you can handle yourself. I just..." He didn't finish the sentence.

"Leon gave me a creepy vibe," I admit as I look again at the bruise. "Is he worse off than you, I hope?"

Marshal's smile is back. "Yeah, I kicked his ass."

"And the slumber party?"

"I wasn't taking a chance on anyone coming back during the night."

"I really do love you," I say with a tired grin.

"Back at you."

I lift my eyebrows. "I could do without the morning wood."

"It was morning," he says pleadingly.

"And your house is gross."

"It's not mine, and I'm moving out at the semester break. Then when you visit, I'll have only one roommate."

"Who?"

"I'm moving in with Drew. His roommate is graduating early."

Finishing my breakfast sandwich, I nod approvingly. "I like Drew. I'll buy you some Lysol as a housewarming gift."

"The only thing that would help where I'm living now is a match."

"I'll get the lighter fluid."

"See," Marshal says, "that's what I like about you. You're willing to go to jail for me."

I look at his bruise. "Well, you just admitted to assault for me. What's a little arson for a friend?"

CHAPTER
Four

Marshal
Six years ago

"*This* weather is shit," my brother, Marcus, says.

I shake my head. "Figures, it's just like Grandpa to pass away during a freak spring snowstorm."

Marcus smiles. "He would hate to have a big celebration of life, wouldn't he?"

"Yeah. He avoided crowds at all costs."

"You boys all right?" my dad asks as he comes up behind us.

Boys.

I'm literally weeks away from my graduation and have a job lined up in Grand Rapids, not terribly far from here, with one of the top architectural firms in the state. Marcus is three years older, married and living near Detroit with a baby on the way. Sally's due date is close, only three weeks away, the same time as my graduation. And her doctor doesn't want her to travel, especially not with the weather.

We turn. "How about you, Dad?" I ask.

"I'm worried about your grandmother. She'll need everyone and with this snow" —he gestured toward the window— "there's no way her and Dad's friends will be able to make it here or the funeral."

"You know that Sally would be here—"

Dad shakes his head at Marcus with a grin. "Sally is where she should be."

"Just think," I say, "soon you'll be a grandpa, Grandpa George."

"Circle of life," he replies softly as he walks toward our mom and his other siblings.

Beyond the window, the snow continues to accumulate.

Hell, on my old truck, I see at least six inches and I've only been at the funeral home for a little more than an hour. This is supposed to be the visitation with the funeral following afterward. So far, it's been only family with a few stragglers from my grandparents' church. I guess it's also my church. I just haven't been in a while.

Life.

Things.

I currently live six hours away.

I notice our grandma standing at the side of the casket, looking down at Grandpa. It's an awful tradition if you ask me. I've never been a fan of funerals. Nevertheless, I make myself walk forward and take a moment since she's alone.

"Grandma," I say as I lay my hand on her lower back.

"Oh, Marshal," she says with a smile. "Do you think he did this?"

"He?"

"Your grandpa?"

Did what...died?

I'm not sure what she means.

"This weather," she says as she takes in my puzzled expression. "It would be just like Lloyd, you know." She lowers her voice. "He never liked funerals or weddings, or well, any gathering. Unless it was a pitch-in. He loved pitch-ins." A smile breaks across her face as she turns to the windows and back. "I can just hear him up in heaven talking to the good Lord and telling him to dump a snowstorm on us. For heaven's sake, it's April." She shakes her head with a smile. "It was Lloyd. I just know it. He's telling me that I should have bypassed all the pomp and circumstance."

"Marcus and I were saying something similar."

She turns and reaches up to my cheek with her cool hand. "You're a good boy, Marshal."

There it is again.

Boy.

Apparently, to family members kids don't grow up.

"When are you going to settle down?"

"You know me, Grandma."

"I do. You're a lot like him" —she peers over at Grandpa— "you know?"

I turn and stare at my grandfather's body.

While it's not really there, I see the smirk on his lips, the way his eyes would sparkle when he'd play a joke or tease. He was always quick with a laugh and even quicker at giving his opinion. I don't mind the comparison.

The door from the vestibule opens, bringing a gust of cool air.

Grandma turns and grins. "Well, lookie there."

I turn and gaze in shock and awe as Sami shakes the snow from her hair and her mom whispers in her ear. Her dad, Paul, is a few steps behind. When Sami looks up, her green eyes meet mine. But instead of talking to me first, she and her parents go straight to my grandma. I watch as first Jean and then Sami reach for my grandma's hand and offer their condolences. With each passing minute, I feel a sense of relief that my grandma has visitors, and at the same time, looking out the window, I want to scold Sami for traveling all the way from Ann Arbor in this weather.

Finally, she comes to me and lifts her arms around my neck. "I'm sorry, Marsh."

"I should kick your ass," I whisper as we hug, "for driving in this weather."

When she steps back, her pretty face has a grin from ear to ear. "You tried that when we were five. I believe I bloodied your nose."

Looking down at all five feet five of her petite frame compared to my six feet three and knowing I outweigh her by at least one hundred and twenty pounds, I shake my head. "You always have been violent."

"Me? You just threatened me."

I reach for her hand. "Seriously, you shouldn't have."

"No, Marsh, I should. When have you ever let me down?"

"Well, there was that one time when I took all your M&M's from your Halloween candy."

Her green eyes open wide. "It was you. I blamed Millie." She soft-punches my arm. "And you let me. You said you'd always tell me the truth."

I nod. "If I remember correctly, you jumped to the Millie conclusion without asking me." I shrug. "I simply didn't correct you. That isn't lying."

She takes a step back and scans me from head to toe. "Just like that dance. You look good in a suit, Marsh."

I do the same, taking in her pretty smile, soft sweater, black slacks, and boots. I shake my head. "I'm glad you didn't wear that red dress. You would have given Grandpa a heart attack, if he hadn't already had one."

"Marsh." She elongates my name. "Are you all right?"

"If I tell you that I'm better with you here, does it make me sound like a pussy?"

"No. It makes you sound like a man who could use his best friend." Her gaze goes to the window and back. "Besides, it's a bit cold for that dress."

Taking her hand, I lead her out of the big room, down a hallway.

"Where are we going?" she asks.

"Trust me?"

Her smile grows. "Always and forever, but..."

I stop. "But?"

"You have a history of getting me in trouble especially back here in Johnson."

"Your memory is playing tricks on you. I think you're the one who instigated most of those incidents."

I tug her hand as we step into a kitchenette area with a table filled with food. Most of the food came from ladies from the church.

"Wow," Sami says as she reaches for a mini-muffin. "The ladies from the church never disappoint."

There was something comforting in not having to explain things to Sami. She just knew.

"Are you nervous?" she asks.

"About Grandpa? I'm worried about Grandma."

She gives me a sad smile. "I mean about graduating and being expected to be adults."

My brow furrows. "Me? I'm never nervous."

"I'm scared shitless." Her lips form an O and her green eyes grow wide as she lowers her head. "Oops. I don't think I'm supposed to say *shit* in a funeral home."

"It's not a church, and no one but me heard you." I lean against the counter. "The advertising firm where you'll be working isn't far from my new office."

Sami smiles. "I'm so glad we'll both be in Grand Rapids. It makes it easier knowing you're there."

"You just drove over six hours in a snowstorm. I think one of us could move to Australia and if the other needed something, we'd be together. In...twenty-four hours."

"You're right. It's just, I imagined being like Marcus." She points toward the room slowly filling with a few brave souls. "He and Sally met at Albion and they knew they'd found their forever. I'm about to graduate. No forever."

"Don't rush it. You'll find him."

"I'm not rushing. I know I'm young, but my parents were married by twenty-one and having kids a few years later."

"Oh my," I say, "I see it now."

"What?"

"You. You're an old maid at twenty-two."

She reaches for her face, palming her cheeks. "Are my wrinkles showing?" Her expression turns. "What about you? Amy really seemed—"

"Clingy," I offer, interrupting her.

"Oh, come on. You talked about her for nearly three months."

I shake my head. "I think it's a serious medical condition." I scratch my neck. "I developed a rash."

Sami's hand goes up. "Oh, no stories about STDs."

I can't help but laugh. "No. I told you I keep it

wrapped. I think that I'm allergic to commitment. She started talking about moving to Grand Rapids and getting an apartment together." I scratch my arms. "See, even talking about it is making me itch."

"You're hopeless."

"But you're not. Give it time."

For the next few hours, hometown friends and cousins join us, and all the while, Sami smiles and talks, knowing everyone. Hell, we all grew up together. It's like old home week until it's time for the ceremony celebrating my grandpa's life.

As we walk into the main room, Sami looks around. I know she's looking for her parents. "Hey," I say as I reach for her hand and lower my voice. "I'm not being a pussy."

"Never."

"Sit with me."

"What about your family?"

"Sit with all of us. I promise they won't mind."

And she does.

I'm not an emotional guy, and I don't do feelings, but even I admit to loving my grandpa. Saying goodbye is one of those things that you know will come but always happens too soon. It's nice having Sami with me, literally holding my hand.

Later, as we gather in the basement of the church, I see the long buffet of food and remember what

Grandma said. I whisper to Sami, "Grandpa did love a good pitch-in."

"Then I say we eat two plates each, just for him."

A smile breaks through my sadness as she reaches for two plates. Hell, half the women I date won't eat a full meal in front of me or any other guy, yet here's Sami, balancing two plates while she fills them with home-made noodles, real mashed potatoes, and freshly canned green beans. "I'll eat brussels sprouts tomorrow," she says as she covers her noodles and potatoes with gravy.

I scan her slim frame. "I don't think you need to worry, and you don't like brussels sprouts."

"Yeah, but I'll have a desk job soon. I need to eat better. I'm going to gain weight and get old."

"Bonus, extra weight will hide your wrinkles."

She grins. "If I wasn't holding two plates, I'd hit you."

"You're always so violent."

"Here take this," she says as she hands me one of her plates.

As soon as I do, she punches my arm. I barely feel it, but it doesn't stop my comeback. "Violent and bossy."

CHAPTER
Five

Sami

Less than one year ago

I can't stop myself from looking at the gorgeous diamond on my left hand. Under the dim lighting of the bar, I wiggle my finger near the candle in the middle of our table.

"Yes, it's beautiful," my friend Linda says before leaning closer, the way she does when she's been drinking.

The truth is that we've all been drinking.

Today, I broke the news of my engagement to Linda, Marcy, and Ashley, all friends of mine from work. I've been at this advertising agency for nearly four years, and when I started, Linda was my godsend, Marcy has the sweetest and most curious disposition, and Ashley started a year after me, and during the week and even on weekends, we've all been inseparable. When I announced my news this morning at work, I had no idea that Linda would call my sisters and arrange an impromptu engagement party.

Ashley lifts her hand in the air. "Another bottle of Moscato," she shouts toward the bar.

Millie, my younger sister, shakes her head. "No, I have to drive back to Johnson." She waves her hand over her nearly empty glass. "I need water."

"No water, wine," Linda says loudly. "Think of it as a miracle, water into wine. And an even greater miracle, Sami here is engaged."

As everyone laughs, including me, I work to fake a pout. "It's not a miracle. It's my forever."

Ashley lifts her glass. "To forever."

"Forever," Marcy says, emptying her glass and wiggling it in the air for more.

Linda tilts her head with a dreamy expression. "Tell us again how Jackson proposed."

I take a deep breath. "On one knee."

"Tell everyone where you were," Millie chimes in.

"We were out to dinner at Sheffield's."

"The country club," Linda adds. "Where he's a member."

"Yeah," I reply, not wanting to flaunt Jackson's money or his position. My fiancé—oh, that was fun to think—just made partner at a big law firm in Grand Rapids. It is all part of his plan—partner at the firm, wife, house, and family. I just am having a tough time believing that I am now a part of that plan. Not only a part. I will be his wife. He will be my husband.

"Do you have a date set?"

"No, Jack doesn't want a long engagement."

"Are we all going to be your bridesmaids?" Ashley asks.

"Who is your maid or matron of honor," Jane, my older sister asks.

"She'll pick me," Millie says with a grin. "I've always been her favorite sister."

"I think she should pick me," Jane replies. "After all, I'm the oldest."

Before I could respond, a deep voice spoke from behind me.

"I think she should pick me."

The entire table turns, mouths agape at the man possessing the voice. I don't need to turn. I'd know that voice anywhere, as well as the firm lips that land on my cheek at the same moment a strong hand lands on my shoulder. "After all, I'm her best friend." He squeezes my shoulder. "Congratulations, Sami."

Nearly spilling my glass of wine, I set it on the table and stand in time to be met with a broad hard chest. I wrap my arms around Marshal's waist and lay my head against that solid torso. When I look up, I blink as his blue eyes shimmer in the bar's illumination. "Why are you here?"

"Because I got a text telling me that my best friend is engaged."

"I texted you yesterday, and you didn't reply."

"So, I'm a shitty best friend."

"No, you're not." I say, my words slurring just a bit.

"Pull up a chair." Jane's direction is repeated by affirmations around the rest of the table.

When I turn, I see my sister's knowing grin. "You told him we were here?" I accuse.

Jane smiles and leans back, lifting her hands. "I did it. I'm guilty as charged."

In the time I've been looking at my older sister, Marshal has pulled up a chair right next to mine. Within seconds, one of the waitresses is at his side, taking his order and probably giving him her phone number. Once she walks away, I turn and lower my voice. With each word, I lean closer and closer, working to keep his blue orbs in focus. "I thought you were upset."

"Upset that my best friend found her forever? Never."

Inhaling, I'm filled with a sense of relief that I hadn't realized I needed. "Thank you."

"So am I going to be your man of honor?"

"Do they do that?" Ashley asks.

"I can do whatever I want," I say. "I'm the bride."

"What is that show?" Linda asks before answering her own question. "Bridezilla."

I lean back, feeling Marsh's arm on the back of my chair and sigh. "I've been imagining this feeling my whole life." I shake my head. "I mean, I have wanted it all, not just *forever*. I want the friends and career. I want a best friend." I squeeze Marshal's knee. "And I want the always." I look at Jane. "You know, like Mom and Dad. And you and Tony." I turn to Millie. "You'll get it one day."

"I'm not worried." She smiles at Marshal. "After all, I know of one guy who's still available."

My younger sister is probably one of the only women in this bar who has no chance of waking in his bed. My sisters and his brother aren't part of our understanding; that was for friends. Siblings are totally and completely off-limits. After all, we all grew up together like stair steps: Jane was the oldest, then Marcus, Marshal's brother, only a few months older than my brother, Byron, and then Marshal and me, and finally Millie.

It would just be weird.

"He's taken," I say as everyone looks my way.

When I turn to Marshal, I smile. "Remember, you told me who you'll end up with?"

"I did?"

"Yeah, right before graduation."

"Who?" Linda asks.

It's as if a light bulb illuminates and Marshal's baby blues open wide. "Sami's right. There's only one person in my forever and it's me."

"Oh," comes from everyone.

"It's okay," he reassures. "That way I can share my attention with everyone."

"I'm free," Linda says with a smirk.

"Nope," I answer. "Friends are off-limits as well as siblings."

"So you're saying as long as I'm friends with you, Marshal is off-limits?"

I know where this is going. "That's our understanding."

"Well, Sami," Linda says, "it's been nice."

We all laugh.

As the night goes on, food continues to be delivered to our table. First there were onion rings and then nachos. The last delivery was a large pizza. It wasn't until we started to disperse that I questioned the tab.

"It's all taken care of," Marshal says.

In the past four years, our financial status has improved.

Marshal's old truck is replaced with a shiny, sleek sports car. My old Camry is now a midsize SUV, and my living arrangement has improved. I have an upscale condo near the river. Marshal also has his own place, high in the sky in a newer building not far from the museum. It's all the rage with coffee shops, delis, and cafes that serve tofu.

"Let me drive you home," he says, plucking my key fob from my hand.

"No." I sway a bit. "I can't leave my car here."

"I'll leave my car. I'll drive you home and Uber back for my car." Marshal lifts his chin toward Jane. "I'll get her home. I promise."

"Thanks, Marsh."

I lower my brow and attempt a scowl. "Did she tell you to come because I was drunk?"

"She mentioned you were celebrating and not eating."

My fist goes to my hip. "Are you, Marshal Michaels, teaming up with Bossy Jane?" It was what we called her when we were kids. Being four years older than us, she felt it was her right to be Mom whenever Mom wasn't about.

Marshal pulls me close, tucking me against him. "The only Anderson on my team is and will always be you, Samantha Ann."

I lean back and stare at his blurry profile. "You used my whole name. I'm in trouble."

"No, you're not in trouble."

It isn't until Marshal has me back in my condo that I ask him what's been on my mind since he didn't return my text message. "You don't like Jack, do you?"

"He's not my forever. He's yours."

I reach out and take Marshal's hand. "I don't want to lose you. I still love you."

"Always and forever?"

I nod. "I just want the other kind of love too. You know the one that takes your breath away and twists your stomach, the one that makes you fall asleep with a smile and wake with one?"

"Honey, if you found that, I will never stand in your

way. Just know that whether you're celebrating your fiftieth anniversary or you need a shoulder, I'm here."

"I know that. I'm here for you too."

I slowly fall to my side and close my eyes, thinking of Jackson, of my friends, of my engagement ring, and how he proposed in front of the entire dining room full of patrons at Sheffield's. My world warms as a blanket comes down over me and firm lips leave a soft kiss on my forehead.

"Do you need an alarm?" Marshal asks.

"My phone—it's always..."

"Let me know when we're going bridesmaid-dress shopping."

I don't see him with my eyes closed, but my cheeks rise as I curl my lips into a smile, and I drift off to sleep.

CHAPTER
Six

Sami

Present

"Oh." My mom's hands go to her lips as her eyes glisten. "It's beautiful, sweetheart. *You're* beautiful."

I loved the dress as I slipped it on in the dressing room, but seeing Mom's reaction tugs at my heart. I spin toward the three-way mirror.

"Come up on the platform," the saleslady says as she fluffs the skirt around me. "You look stunning, Sami. Your mom is right."

I crane my neck over my shoulder, taking in the lace and long line of buttons. The sweetheart neckline does a great job complementing my breasts without emphasizing them. It's the dress I always imagined, but then I remember the price tag.

"Maybe I should try on some other ones?" I say, pitching slightly from side to side, enjoying the full skirt while taking in the intricate details.

Mom steps up on the podium and wraps her arm

around my waist. Her eyes meet mine in the mirror. "Sami, this is *your* wedding. I know what you're thinking, but your dad and I have prepared for this since you and your sisters were young. If this is the dress you want, it's the dress I want you to have."

I lean my head toward her shoulder.

My parents were married and began having children when they were younger than I am now. Seeing her next to me, it's easy to understand how we're mistaken for sisters. My mom is the epitome of understated grace. I grin at her blue jeans and top. Even in her early fifties, she rarely wears much makeup or is excessive about her hair. She and Dad live in the same four-bedroom ranch where they raised four children. They attend the same church and are members of the local Moose Lodge.

In some ways, it's as if they're stuck in time, and in others ways it's obvious that they don't need to change or move up. They're both content. Now, my dad does have an unhealthy obsession with reality television shows and zombies, but other than that, I would say that if you had to define my parents in one word it was content.

"Mom, I know Jackson has ideas for the wedding, and I want you to know, he's willing to contribute. After all, it's *our* wedding."

"Samantha Ann, we paid for Jane's wedding. We'll take care of yours as well as Millie's one day." She squeezes my waist. "I think it's wonderful that Jackson has ideas, but honey, you're the bride. Tell me if you want this dress."

I scan my reflection and imagine my hair styled, my makeup done, and then this dress. With each inch I see, the more in love with the dress I am. "I do."

"Then this is the dress we're getting. And the pearls will be beautiful with the neckline."

By the pearls, she means a family heirloom and tradition.

I don't answer her, knowing Jackson isn't thrilled with the idea of me wearing what he calls hand-me-down jewelry for the wedding. I haven't brought myself to tell my mother. I know how disappointed she'll be. Every female descendant of my great-grandmother has worn the same pearls. My sister Jane was the last.

I should be the next.

As we were talking to the saleswoman, Mom gave her address instead of mine. "Wait."

Mom turns and speaks quietly. "Now that Jackson has moved into your condo..."

"*Our* condo," I correct.

"It's yours and he's there," she replies matter-of-factly. "I understand the reasoning for his move, and so does your dad. But since he's there, I'd rather anything wedding-related come to my email or our address." She smiles and gives my arm a squeeze. "Remember, he isn't supposed to see the dress until he sees you walking down the aisle."

Jackson had moved into my condo shortly after proposing.

Remember the plan: partnership, wife, house...

Well, we've been looking at houses. The market is crazy. The ones we like are gone before we have a chance to see them or make an offer. Last month, we met with one of the area's top builders. Now we are looking at land.

I never considered all the qualifying factors for residency.

Jackson doesn't want to be in the country. He wants a neighborhood that fits our status. He researches everything down to schools and per capita median income. After all, it's important for our children to make the right friends.

Honestly, the subject has lost its luster.

The last time we spoke about land, we got into a big discussion about moving closer to Johnson. Admittedly, outside of my hometown is more rural, but I didn't see that as a bad thing. Apparently, living in Johnson would limit...well, everything. I hadn't realized how deep his negativity of my hometown ran.

He grew up in an upscale neighborhood near Detroit. It's where his parents still live. Just because two of my parents' house could fit in his parents' home, doesn't make it better.

He did find a neighborhood near Sheffield's Country Club that has recently opened up new lots. They won't be ready to build for another six months, which means moving will be at least a year away. According to Jackson, living close to the country club will give us and our children access to perks such as tennis and swimming lessons.

I recall falling to sleep thinking about swimming lessons. Of course, everyone should know how to swim. It's important. However, I couldn't recall not knowing how. Instead of lessons, my siblings and I, Marshal, Marcus, and our friends simply jumped into the deep end or off the cliff at the lake.

"Sami," Mom says as she secures her coat and steps toward the door to the bridal shop. "How about lunch?"

"I should go to the gym, but we can do lunch first."

"Samantha Ann, you're beautiful. Now don't lose more weight. After all, they took your measurements today. We want the dress to fit and show off your beautiful curves."

"That's what alterations are for."

Instead of staying in the city, Mom begins driving away from civilization and toward Johnson. Snow mounds line the country roads where the plows have pushed it out of the way. Today the sun is shining, but this time of year, it does little to warm the air. "Where are we going?"

"Home."

CHAPTER
Seven

Sami

"Home? Mom, you should have dropped me off at my place. I can get my car. Now you'll need to drive me back."

She waves a hand in the air. "Sami, you're about to be a married woman. I don't mind an extra hour with you when I can get it. Besides, the invitations came in and I want you to see them."

"What about the caterers?"

"I need to check with you and Jackson for your schedules and then we can make appointments to try their food."

As we drive and discuss the wedding, I teeter between excitement and guilt. Mom can say what she wants, but I know without a doubt that this wedding is costing more than Jane's. When we arrive at my parents' house, Dad is home.

"What are you doing here?" I ask.

Dad gives me a kiss on the cheek. "Did something happen?" He turns to Mom. "Are you kicking me out?"

"You'll know when I do," she says with a grin. "I'll change the locks."

"Eating lunch, sweetheart. How was dress shopping?" Dad pauses the recording he's watching. "Did you find the perfect dress?"

"I found one."

"What's the matter?" His eyes narrow with concern.

"Dad, please let Jack and I help with the cost."

He shakes his head. "You're our little girl."

"I'm not. I'm an adult with a job and money. Jackson has—"

Dad shakes his head. "Can you please let an old man do what he wants? I've lived with four women, and it's about time they let me have my way."

I giggle. "Are you sure?"

"I'm sure that if I don't finish this recording in the next seventeen minutes, I'll be late for the rest of my day. I have three more classes and the teacher shouldn't be tardy." He shakes his head. "Freshman English. Let me find out who she chooses. It will give me strength to face those kids."

My dad has been at Johnson High School since I was born. He's the head of the English department and is always at work at least two hours early. He's that teacher who makes himself available for help before or after school. His only request is a long enough lunch to go home and watch one of his shows. As I said, he's obsessed with reality television.

Mom offers Dad her phone. "Look, Paul."

My dad's eyes glisten. "Oh, Sami, you're radiant." He narrows his gaze as he looks up. "You're not knocked-up, are you?"

"Dad."

"Good. We want the dress to fit."

Why is everyone worried about the dress fitting?

It isn't until we're on our way to my car that I say, "You could drop me off at the gym, and I'll walk to my car."

Mom sighs. "You've been working out a lot."

"And I'm getting married in four months."

"You were just fitted for your dress today. You don't want to lose too much."

"After the lunch you just fed me," I say with a grin, remembering her homemade chicken salad and the flaky croissant, "I don't think losing too much is possible." It's then I remember the dinner with Jackson's partners. "Shit, Mom. Take me to my car."

"What is it?"

"I forgot that Jackson and I are having dinner tonight with Fred and Martha Wilson."

"As in *Wilson et al?*"

Mr. Wilson is the founding partner of the Wilson et al Law Firm.

"Yeah, them."

"Oh, how fun."

"It's a bit stuffy." I turn to the window and watch as

we get back to the city. My SUV is where we left it at the bridal boutique. Between school buses and afternoon traffic, it takes me longer than I expected to get to our condo.

Instead of taking the elevator, I decide to hurry up the ten flights of stairs to the level of our condo. Taking off my coat, I take the stairs two at a time. I guess I figure it's the workout I haven't gotten. It isn't until I open the door and see Jack's stare as he's standing in his custom suit that my elation for the day completely evaporates.

It isn't Jack's appearance that quells my enthusiasm. He's a handsome man in a dignified way. Only in his mid-thirties, he has just a few strands of gray hair, the amount that makes a man look distinguished. He works out regularly, and I know that under that fancy suit is a toned and fit body.

"Where have you been?" He looks me up and down. "Wearing that?"

I'm wearing a pair of long workout pants and a shirt with a sports bra. When I'd dressed I'd planned on going from the bridal boutiques to the gym. "With my mom. You knew we were shopping for wedding dresses," I say as I toss my coat and purse on a chair. I look up at the clock. "It's only four. Our reservations aren't until six. I'll be ready."

"Did you even look at your phone?"

I hadn't.

"Why?"

"Fred wants to meet for drinks at five."

"Shit, I'm sorry, Jack. I was shopping for my wedding dress. Remember, we're getting married."

"I'm well aware, Samantha." He shakes his head. "Do you even care about my position at the firm?"

"You're a partner. Are they going to take that away?"

He shakes his head, takes a deep breath, and walks toward me. He reaches for my upper arms and pulls me toward him, leaving an attention-getting kiss on my lips. "I know finding the right dress is important," he says, his tone mellowing as he still holds onto my arms. "Did you find one?"

"I did."

"I hope you went to a boutique and not one of those stores where you buy one off the rack."

"We went to a boutique, Jack. You try the dresses on from the rack. I found one that Mom and I both liked. Now they will make one to fit my measurements."

"You told them that you've been working out? I mean, we don't want it to be too loose."

For some reason, coming from him it felt different than the way it felt when my mom had said the same thing.

"I told them."

"How is Jean?"

"She's good. I saw Dad too."

"He was there?"

"No, Mom took me back to their house for lunch. The invitations came in. They're perfect."

His brown eyes narrow. "You didn't work out?"

"I ran the stairs, Jack."

He nods. "How about I Uber to the restaurant, explain to Fred and Martha that you've been shopping for your wedding dress, and you drive over and arrive by six?"

He made it sound like an option, but it felt as though it was my only one. "I'm sorry. I should have checked—"

Jack's lips land on mine. "It will work out fine. I'll see you at six."

"I'll be there."

As he starts to walk away, he turns and pulls his key fob from his pocket. "Samantha, drive my car."

Of course, his BMW would look better as we drive away than my SUV.

"And since you've been running around and busy, I thought I'd help. I laid out a dress for you to wear. You'll be stunning."

I grit my teeth and keep my smile intact. "That was very thoughtful of you."

"It was. You're welcome."

CHAPTER *Eight*

Marshal

*O*ur architectural firm just landed a coveted project that includes four new hotels, two in Michigan and two in Pennsylvania. There is this hotel mogul who is looking to expand further, so if he and his board are happy with our final results, this partnership could be life changing for us.

I say *us*, but I'm not a partner. However, it was my designs that got the hotel mogul interested, the one that caught his eye. That said, I'm part of a team. Tonight, my team is celebrating on the company's dime. Hell, The Rooftop is one of the nicest restaurants in Grand Rapids and one with the biggest price tags.

"Marshal," the owner and CEO of our architectural firm, Jason McMann, says as he pats my back. "What can we get you for a before-dinner drink? As you know, I'm a whiskey man myself."

"I'm a bourbon fan. I like it smooth."

Jason grins. "I bet you do." He turns to the pretty thing behind the bar. "Barbie" —yes, that is her name.

It's on a small pin-on tag right over her large left boob—
"can you get my friend Marshal two fingers of Blanton's."
He turns back to me. "On the rocks?"

"Neat." My answer comes without emotion as I stare
across the bar and clench my teeth.

This restaurant has one of those modern open-
concept bars.

If it were warmer outside, the glass windows would
be opened and there would be tables on the balcony
overlooking the river and the city lights. As it is, the
windows are closed, keeping the snow and wind outside.
However, the bar is open. Blue lighting projects around
the center cabinetry where hundreds of bottles are
proudly displayed. From where I'm standing, I can see to
the other side, to a group of people.

They're dressed much as we are, in nice business
attire. The women are a bit dressier. I can't see below
their waists, but I know a woman's body well enough to
know the way one walks in tall heels. There's a rhythm
to the way their bodies sway, as if they are asking for a
strong hand to support them.

No, I wouldn't take only their sway as an invitation.

Nearly a decade post-high school and I'm no more
committed to a relationship than before, but I'm also
not in danger of a sexual harassment lawsuit. I believe in
consent.

For once, though, I'm not looking at a woman but at
a man.

My jaw clenches tighter as a slimy smile curls his lips, and he whispers something to a woman I don't recognize. One might wonder why it would matter to me that a man is speaking to a woman at too close of a distance. It does because that man is engaged to my best friend.

"Marshal," Jason says as he hands me a glass and others from our office gather around. Jason turns to all of us. There are three men and four women. We're the team that worked on the bid. We're the team that just landed Jason the biggest (and potentially even bigger) deal he's ever had. "You did it. Thank you," he says.

We all clink our glasses.

The bar is getting more crowded as we wait for our table.

"Do you know Jackson Carmichael?" Melinda Beavo, a very talented architect and member of our group and a married woman, asks quietly, following my line of vision.

"Is it that obvious?"

"You've been staring at him for the last fifteen minutes."

"Do you know him?" I ask, keeping my voice and anger at bay.

"A little. I'm not a member of his fan club, but from what little interaction I've had with him, I believe it's a club of one."

She makes me smirk. "So you do know him."

"My husband has done some work with their law firm. My connection is distant, but I've had enough encounters to know he is a conceited piece of..." She lifts her glass of red wine to her smiling lips. After taking a drink, she asks, "Why do you care?"

"His fan club has recently inducted a new member. He's engaged."

"To that blonde over there, the one he's been schmoozing with since we arrived?"

"Nope," I say matter-of-factly.

"How well do you know his fiancée?"

I like Melinda. She's maybe ten years my senior and has worked hard for her place in our firm, yet she's never talked down or acted like she knew more than any of the newer members. She's been open to our ideas while willing to point out her own. She's a team player, which is about the best compliment I could give anyone. I look directly at Melinda. "His fiancée is my friend. I've known her...forever." I shrug. "She's probably my best friend."

"That explains why you look like you want to punch something."

My poor teeth are ready to splinter as I increase the pressure. "I was thinking more of some*one*." I look around the bar, but Sami is nowhere to be found. "I want the piece of shit to know I'm here."

"You could yell across the bar, but I suggest a more direct approach."

I look at our group, all chatting and smiles. This is an occasion that deserves celebration. However, my thoughts are consumed with what I'm seeing. I can't hear what Carmichael and the blonde are saying, but I'm not naive. I'm about as far from it as one can get. I recognize the moves, the body language, the fluttering of her hands and the way he leans in to speak.

Fuck, I perfected those moves.

"Melinda, if anyone asks, will you tell them that I went to speak to a *friend* and I'll be right back?"

"Friend?" Her eyes narrow. She reaches for my arm and leans closer. "Be open-minded." When she releases me, she grins. "See, that—my touching your arm and leaning toward you—was innocent, but from across the bar..."

"Yeah, sure." Melinda's touch lasted maybe five seconds. I've been watching Carmichael for over fifteen minutes. "I'm very open-minded."

Open-minded that Jackson Carmichael is a horse's ass.

With each step, I remind my heart to slow and my blood pressure to calm. I haven't felt this protective of Sami since college when there was an asshole at a party making his moves on her. Thankfully, he never pressed charges. I'd heard he sported a black eye for a bit. As I neared the group of people, I reminded myself that Sami thought of Carmichael as her forever.

She'd also considered Todd and Josh to name a few.

Josh turned out to be a good guy. He was hired by the Lions. It also happened that after he moved away from Ann Arbor, he discovered what he hadn't been willing to admit. Josh prefers men to women. A smile comes to my lips as I remember the way Sami took it.

God, she was great.

Last I heard, she and Josh are still good friends.

She's dated other men along the way, but none of them had put a ring on her finger.

As I rounded the end of the bar, my gaze went from the snow-covered balcony to the dark-haired man at the bar. By the change of his expression, he saw me too.

"Michaels," Carmichael said with a nod and a sobering expression. "What are you doing here?"

I straightened my shoulders and utilized every inch of my height. "It's a bar." I lifted my tumbler. "I'm having a drink. What are you doing here? And" —I nodded at the blonde, who was now scanning me in a way I recognize— "who is your date?"

Carmichael bristled. "This is our newest intern, Ellen Modarski. Ellen, this is Marshal Michaels."

She lifted her hand my direction. "Very nice to meet you."

"We're waiting for our table." Carmichael's gaze goes behind me as he tries to make himself appear taller. "And here's my date."

As if she materializes out of thin air, Sami steps around me, reaching for her fiancé's outstretched hand.

"Jack, I'm sorry I'm late."

She hands him a key fob. "No valet. I parked it myself."

Jack nods, taking the fob from her.

Before she realizes I am even there, I have a flashback of a dance and a red dress. Hell, the one she is wearing now covers about as much skin as that red one did back then. In her defense, this one is cut differently, not as revealing on top, but damn, how did she walk on the icy sidewalk in those shoes?

Sami spins my direction, her smile wavering and recovering. "Marsh, what's going on?"

The knot in my chest pulls tighter as I force a smile. I want to tell her the truth. That's always been our thing. But do I really know the truth? Maybe Melinda is right. Maybe it was all innocent. I clear my throat. "I'm here with some of my coworkers celebrating a big deal and saw Carmichael. I stopped to say hi."

Carmichael nods. "I heard McMann landed the Sirius Hotel deal." He extends his hand. "Congratulations. I should buy you a drink."

I force myself to take his hand. "No, thank you." I turn to Sami. "Hey gorgeous, how about lunch sometime?"

"I've never been able to turn you down."

When Ellen looks from Sami to me and back, I feel the need to save my best friend, to protect her. I'm not sure if it's necessary, but I can't stop myself. "Old friends," I explain.

"Since you were five?" Carmichael says in the form of a question.

"Since Sami kicked my ass. Watch out. She has a mean right hook." Sami's smile warms my heart, slowly unknotting my worries.

"I'll text you," she says before turning to Ellen and talking to her, completely unaware that moments earlier that woman was flirting with—no, her fiancé was flirting with that woman.

I can't say I feel better as I walk away, but I don't feel worse.

Did I just save Sami from witnessing what I'd been watching?

If I did, is that good or bad?

By the time I make it back to the others from my firm, I've chosen to believe it is all innocent and good. I glance across the bar to see her smile. It lights up the entire room. If Sami stood closer to the windows, she would undoubtedly melt the snow.

"Are you all right?" Melinda asks as we follow a hostess to our table.

"I think so."

CHAPTER
Nine

Marshal

"No, no..." Sami's words trail away as she shakes her head.

It's been a little over three months since the incident at the bar and seeing the hurt in Sami's expression and the tears on her cheeks, I know I made the wrong choice that night. I won't do the same tonight.

The bourbon burns as I take a long sip.

The alcohol doesn't dull her pain, but it helps calm my rage at myself and her no-good asshole ex.

Ex as in she left her engagement ring on the kitchen counter of her condo before coming here.

Even half-wasted, Sami is adorable. I love the way her long, wavy hair becomes curly in the summer's heat. She hates it. She always has, but I can't stop myself from reaching out and tweaking a long chestnut curl, just to watch it bounce.

"Stop it!" she says, pulling away and laying her head against my sofa.

Her eyes half close and the glass of wine in her hand tips one way and then the other.

"Sami, let me take that," I offer as I reach for the wine.

Her grip on the long stem tightens.

"No. I'm going to drink this wine. I'm going to drink all" —her arms fly open wide as I capture the glass once more. This time I seize the glass as the liquid sloshes and just before my light brown leather sofa has a nice red stain— "the wine you have." Her plump lips purse and change to a pout when she realizes the glass is gone. "Fine, take the glass, only because I know you're going to refill it for me. Aren't you, Marshal? You wouldn't let me stay sober, not after..."

Her words trail away as more tears fall from the corners of her green eyes.

"He's not worth it." It's the same thing I've told her fifty times since she got to my apartment. "He's not worth the wine or the headache you're going to have in the morning. He's a slime. A douche. An asshole. And coming from one asshole, I know assholes. I never knew what you saw in him anyway."

Her arms cross over her tits, not in anger but in the way she does to protect herself, shield herself from everyone else.

Placing my glass and her wine on the end table, I tug on one of her hands and shine my cockiest grin.

"Besides, wouldn't you rather be here with me than with him?"

I've grabbed her left hand.

I hadn't meant to.

It was just the closest.

We both look down at her empty ring finger. Just a few hours ago she'd been wearing a giant diamond engagement ring.

Sami pulls her hand back and her words slur. "We were supposed to be married."

No longer sad, she springs up from the couch.

In only a moment, she changes from jilted fiancée to the Sami I've known most of my life, the one who wouldn't let some asshole walk all over her, and the one who's been my best friend for the last twenty-three years. Finally pulling herself out of her wine-induced funk, she staggers before catching herself by holding the back of a chair. Standing tall, she says, "In three weeks." She holds up three fingers, narrows her eyes as she concentrates on them and then repeats, "Three."

"Sami." I lift my hand, palm up, toward her.

She shakes her head and opens her eyes wide. "Holy shit," she continues, "do you have any idea how much money my parents are spending on this wedding? Have spent? As in money they probably can't get back? Shit. My mom. Oh my God, my mom has been working so hard. She's going to have a coronary. And my dad, holy shit, Marshal, he may never recover."

I stand ready to catch her if she wobbles again.

With her green eyes glistening, Sami stares up at me, silently demanding an answer.

"I don't know how much they've spent. But I know they won't be as upset as you think."

Her green eyes narrow.

"Sami, they hate his guts."

"No, they don't," she answers defensively. "They love him. Everybody" —she elongates the word— "loves Jack. Jack and Sami. Sami and Jack. The perfect couple."

"Jack isn't perfect. He's far from it. Don't forget, he's the asshole who fucked some other woman in your bed."

"It was her."

"Her who?"

"Ellen." Sami's nose scrunches. "She's that intern at their practice—the one you met at The Rooftop bar. Jack told me he was assigned to watch over her work. Apparently, watching over means screwing her from above."

I shake my head. "Listen to me. Your dad would have voted Jackson off the island a long time ago."

A smile comes to my lips just thinking of her dad's obsession with reality television and zombies.

If there were a reality zombie show, he'd be set for life—or the apocalypse. If the apocalypse happens, after his years of watching *Survivor* and *The Walking Dead*, among hundreds of others, I'll definitely want him on my team. I already have him programmed in my phone, for phone-a-friend, just in case.

According to Paul, you should always be prepared.

Who knows? One day I may find myself on the set of some game show that asks obscure questions related to reality television, English grammar, and zombies. If that happens, I'm prepared.

Sami takes a deep breath. "No, he wouldn't. Dad was thrilled that I was marrying Jack. And well, no one knows about that Ellen thing—no one but you and of course Jack and her." She nods her head. "Yep, that's everyone. Hell, they were so into it, I doubt they even know I was there."

I run my hands over her arms, up and down. "You should have grabbed a lamp and conked them both upside the head."

A smile tugs at the corner of her lips. "That's why I love you. Violence is always your first thought."

I shrug. "I'd say it's yours. Usually screwing is my first thought. But...well, that was already happening."

She playfully hits my shoulder. "Thanks for the reminder."

"Ouch. See. Be violent with Jack, not with me."

As I wrap my arms around my best friend, she falls against my chest. The scent of strawberries tickles my nose, and I take a deeper breath. For just a second, Sami seems to relax and melt against me. Our friendship has seen it all. We know each other's deepest, darkest secrets and we're still here—through childhood, our teens, college, and now.

Always.

The one thing we haven't done, not ever, is move beyond friendship. It is our most important agreement, one we made when we were young. We also agreed that friends and family were off-limits. I crossed that line once but learned my lesson. As for the line between me and Sami, we've stayed true.

Keeping that line in place was easy when we were running around the neighborhood or swimming in the lake. Back then it was as if we were brother and sister, but sometimes lately the thought crosses my mind. After all, that agreement was between two kids. Sami is definitely no longer a kid and neither am I. I sometimes wonder what it would be like to be with Sami, *with* her, making love with her.

But I can't do it. I won't.

No matter how beautiful she has become, or fun, or happy, or sad, we are friends first and always. We can't jeopardize that. However, if we did cross that line, I'm sure I could help her forget that asshole Jack.

No. Her friendship is worth more than finding out how great we'd be together.

Besides, it isn't like I'm living a life of abstinence. I get plenty of action.

I've taken many women places they didn't know they could go, all in the name of forgetting some asshole who wronged them. But that won't be how I help Sami.

Earlier tonight, when I got Sami's hysterical call, I was on my way to a date. The *date* was just drinks with some chick from the gym. We've talked a few times. Her name starts with K or a C. I can't remember. It's like Katie or Catlin. All I know for sure is that she has great tits and a nice ass and wears excessively tight clothing to the gym. When she invited me for drinks, I didn't think about saying no.

I also didn't get her number.

Now I'm the douche guy who stood her up.

Remembering her body, they way her tits bounce when she runs on the treadmill, I'm most certain that she won't be alone for long. And since I can't remember her name, I'm not too brokenhearted.

I reassure my libido that the next time I see Miss Tits and Ass at the gym, all I'll need to do is flash my baby blues, wipe the sweat from my forehead with my shirt, showing off my tight abs, and claim that a heart-broken friend kept me away. Then I'll ask if we can reschedule. Ten to one says she won't hold a grudge for long.

After all, what's more appealing than a good-looking, successful guy who went to a friend's rescue?

Tonight is about Sami.

Besides, the chick from the gym gives off the same vibe I do. She's not looking for anything other than some fun and a good time. Those have been my goals forever, but the order of significance is most usually reversed.

Sami and I have always had different life goals. Yet, in most ways, we're both living the dream.

It's just that our dreams for a relationship—a forever, until-I-die thing—have always been different.

My mind goes through her list of boyfriends, ending with the slime bag, Jack. From the time we were young, I've wanted her to find her forever. She thought she had. Unfortunately, as my shirt continues to dampen with her tears, Sami's forever just screwed his intern—in Sami's bed.

"Hey, how about I order some dinner," I offer. "I can have sushi here in twenty minutes."

Sami sighs against my chest. "I deserve better." Her voice is soft but determined.

"You sure as hell do. We'll make it pizza and breadsticks with the little containers of gooey cheese."

"No." She tips her chin upward until our eyes meet. "I'm not talking about food. I deserve to be happy."

That's my girl. "And sushi is the perfect start."

I suck in a breath as she reaches down, purposely rubbing the front of my jeans.

"What are you doing?" Though I'm asking the question, I'm well aware of what she's doing. This isn't my first rodeo.

Sami blinks. Her tears have dried, and her damn

green eyes are filled with something I've never seen before, not from her. Her cheeks rise as her pink tongue darts out to her lip and then disappears. "I think I have a better idea than food, something that will make me feel better."

CHAPTER
Ten

Sami

*W*hat *the hell am I doing?*

My heart is racing, and all I can think about is Marshal. Of course I'm thinking about the way his chest feels against mine, how strong and sturdy it is. I'm thinking about his arms and how he surrounds me, protecting me from the world.

But those aren't necessarily new thoughts. I mean, we've been friends forever, since long before he was sexy as hell and six feet plus. Sometimes to me, he's still the short, freckle-faced boy who lives down the street. I'm not alone in the way I see him or us. I know he still thinks of me as that little girl.

Time moves on...we've grown up.

I know we made an agreement, but so did Jack and I. We'd agreed to marry.

I wonder if that asshole has found my engagement ring on the kitchen counter yet or if he's still too busy screwing that bimbo. I've turned off my phone so I don't have a clue if he's tried to call. Furthermore, I don't give a shit. After what I saw, he can go screw himself or anyone else. All I know for sure is that it won't be me.

Which brings me back to the man with his arms around me. The man who I know—through his own and others' testimonials—is rumored to be fantastic in bed.

Jack was okay.

But damn it, I deserve better.

I deserve fantastic.

We can do this, I convince myself.

Marshal and I can cross this line and then go back to the way it was. Hell, maybe we don't have to go back to the way it was. Maybe we can stay friends and keep...

Yes.

Friends with benefits.

Why not?

My mind is a flurry of thoughts.

I love the man with his arms around me, and I don't want to do what I've accused him of doing—use someone. That thought lingers and fades.

No. This wouldn't be that.

I'm not trying to get even with Jack. I'm not.

Maybe for the first time I'm recognizing what's been in front of me forever and always. I lift my lips to Marshal's as I reach out and stroke his jeans.

Once.

Twice.

With each stroke, his cock grows larger and harder under the fabric.

He says something again about food.

"I think I have a better idea than food, something that will make me feel better."

"Sami..."

My two-syllable name becomes a full four as Marshal's eyes roll back and he lowers his head until his forehead rests on mine.

"Marshal Michaels, don't make me beg. I deserve this. You deserve this. I'm a damn good lay. I promise."

"Don't say that. We...we have our agreement."

I continue stroking his cock, the bulge in his jeans growing bigger and bigger. Harder and harder. He doesn't try to stop me as his chest rises and falls.

"I propose a new agreement," I say with confidence. But then as I reach for the buckle of his belt, Marshal stops me.

"Honey, you know I love you."

"And I love you. I have since we were five."

Marshal's cheeks rise. "You sure had a funny way of showing it."

I shrug at the memory. With pink filling my cheeks, I concede, "Okay. Since we were six, then. Now we're both adults. We can do this and still be friends. I'm not wanting more—I'm done with forever. It doesn't really exist. Right now, I just want to *feel*. I want to be close to someone."

"I'm here."

"You know what I mean." When he doesn't respond,

I ask, "Do you really want me to get what I need at some bar from a stranger? Because I'm getting it tonight."

His arms tense and I know I've hit a nerve.

"Don't act like that makes me something I'm not. When was the last time you didn't get laid when you wanted to?"

Marshal's Adam's apple bobs. "You're killing me here."

I look up at his blue orbs, seeing the way they swirl with indecision. He's my best friend and protector. If I would let him, instead of being here with me, he'd be at our condo and Jack would be beaten to a bloody pulp.

Our condo.

My stomach drops. It's *my* condo, and Jack can get his ass out.

"No," Marshal says, "I don't want you at a bar with a stranger, but, Sami..."

I take a step back and reach for the hem of my shirt. Pulling it over my head, I watch as Marshal's blue eyes grow in proportion to his cock as his gaze is suddenly glued to my boobs. They're big and round and pushed upward in my pink Victoria's Secret bra. "Either I'm going to crawl into your bed and have a sleepover with my best friend" —I reach for the button on my jeans— "or my best friend is going to need to tell me to leave, and I guess I'll look for somewhere else to stay because I sure as hell can't go back to my condo tonight."

Marshal runs his hand through his light brown hair as he watches my next move.

"What will it be?" I shimmy out of my jeans and leave them on his floor near my shirt. "Are you going to kick me out?"

"I don't want to be a get-even fuck, Sami."

My head tilts to the side. "Really? You've never been in this situation before?"

"Not with you. You're different."

Marshal Michaels has never turned down sex, no matter the reason.

I take a deep breath, reach up, and stroke his chiseled jaw. "I don't want this to get even." My head shakes. "Jack can screw whomever he wants. What I want isn't about him. It's about me. And" —I separate each word for emphasis— "This. Won't. Change. A. Thing."

"Our agreement?" he asks again with more uncertainty in his voice.

"Let's have a new agreement?"

For only a moment, I remember all the effort, all the working out, to be ready for my wedding and honeymoon and decide I want to show off my toned body to my best friend. Wearing only my bra and matching boy shorts—the kind that show off my butt cheeks—I reach for Marshal's hand. I've never noticed before how big it is. How long his fingers are. How strong his grasp is.

I take a step toward his bedroom.

It's only one step, but suddenly, I'm pulled back into

his arms. My waist is pulled tight against him, his erection grinding against me and probing the flesh of my stomach.

I wince as Marshal tugs my hair, forcing my head backward until I'm staring up into his eyes.

My breathing hitches as I take him in. The blue is different, deeper, stronger, and there's something new.

"Tell me you're sure."

The crotch of my panties dampens.

"Marshal..."

"No, Sami. Tell me."

I try to swallow. In the last few seconds, breathing has become more difficult.

Shit.

"I-I'm sure," I say, my answer squeaking out.

What just happened?

I wanted to feel close to my friend. I wanted the togetherness that Jack's stupid escapade took away. I wanted a *friend*. But now? Shit, now I'm turned on. My core clenches and my circulation quickens.

I've never seen this side of Marshal, the sexy side that others have seen. Now that I have, I want more.

Before I can say anything else, Marshal pushes me backward until my shoulders collide with the wall and he's against me, all of him.

I moan as his stiff cock pushes harder against my stomach.

"Fuck, Sami, I'm not sure what's happening, but I

don't do sleepovers, not anymore. I don't do sweet. Not when it comes to sex. You know me."

My nipples harden as he crushes my breasts against his chest. "I know you, Marshal, better than anyone. Take me. I want to be consumed. I want my mind so focused on you, on here, and on now that the rest of the world fades away." I fight emotion I don't want to feel and concentrate on the man before me. "Marshal, I want to think about only you, the one man who's never lied to me."

His eyes narrow. "And tomorrow?"

"You'll still be my best friend."

Marshal reaches down and unashamedly moves the crotch of my panties. I bite my lip as he plunges one and then two fingers deep inside me. The room fills with his growl, guttural and primitive. He isn't the only one making sounds. With each plunge I moan with pleasure.

"Fuck, Sami, you're so wet. You really do want this, don't you?"

My core tightens around his long fingers, and my knees weaken as I move with his rhythm. "More than my dad wants the apocalypse." I move on my toes, finding his rhythm. My voice is breathy as I say, "Please, Marshal, don't make me beg."

CHAPTER
Eleven

Marshal

Thoughts I've never let myself think are rushing through my mind.

With each plunge of my fingers, my imagination runs wild.

I picture Sami begging—my Sami on her knees pleading for my cock.

I want that.

I want *that* and more.

The surge of desire overwhelms me. She is like nothing I've ever imagined having for my own in my entire life. Then again, she's the one who's always been there, the one who knows me, my friend.

The need for more is coursing through my bloodstream, electrifying every nerve ending, and intensifying my senses. I feel every inch of her beneath me, my chest on hers, and my erection against her stomach. The way her silky, wet pussy squeezes my fingers, I can't imagine what it will do to my dick. And damn, the noises she's making are echoing off the walls.

How is it possible to want somebody so badly when that somebody has always been near?

Images I never entertained are creating an erotic slideshow in my mind.

Sami writhing beneath me.

Sami on her knees as her pink tongue darts out to lick my rock-hard dick.

I imagine watching her lips as I fist her hair and she takes me deep into her throat. I hear her gasping for air as her head bobs up and down. My cock aches thinking about her taking me, all of me, until I come and she swallows every last drop. I don't want to stop there. If this goes a second more, I won't stop.

I want to slide inside her core and feel those warm walls clench around me like they are doing to my fingers.

My brain is saying *no*.

It's saying all the words that mean *no*.

Such as stop.

And don't do this.

And this isn't a good idea.

My brain is saying that this new agreement will never work. It's telling me to tuck my friend into my bed and move to the couch. It's telling me to jack off in the bathroom and forget this ever happened.

I've never been good at listening to my brain.

Especially not when another part of my anatomy is in on the debate.

I lean forward and take her lips, capture them, claim

them. My brain says to be gentle, to merely brush our lips as friends do. Fuck my brain. All self-control is quickly fleeing. Gentle isn't in my vocabulary.

Twenty-plus years of being gentle with Sami are suddenly washed away by a flood of desire, much like the flood saturating my pumping fingers. I push closer, bruising her lips, making them red and puffy. As I do, a soft whimper escapes Sami's mouth. It's just the encouragement I need as I plunge my tongue between her lush lips.

Her warm mouth is ecstasy. It's sweet, like grapes, while also tart like wine. The lethal combination enters my system, erasing all sense of right and wrong.

My brain tries one more time: this is Sami, Samantha Anderson, the girl down the street, my best friend. Remember when we were kids...

I shut it down.

That knowledge and definition of this hotter-than-hell vixen quickly morphs to the woman in my apartment, in my arms, and grinding against me.

My body is no longer reasoning or listening to my mind. It's on a path of no return as Sami's heartbeat quickens, her moans fill the room, and her slick pussy clenches again, covering my fingers in more of her honey.

My God. Her pussy is heaven.

Who the fuck knew?

Her mouth is paradise.

How did I never know?

And her body...those tits are sublime.

I release her gorgeous hair and unsnap her bra.

Pulling the straps over her slender shoulders and down her arms, I toss the material onto the floor. "Holy fuck, Sami. How have you kept this gorgeous rack hidden from me?" I lean down and suck one of her nipples into my mouth and run my tongue around the hard bead.

She doesn't answer. Instead, she whimpers as she weaves her fingers through my hair and pulls me closer, arching her back. The pressure is perfect.

Her hip against my dick.

Her tit in my mouth.

Her pussy squeezing my fingers as I pump harder and faster.

Her entire body tenses.

"Marshal, shit. I'm going to come."

"Not yet." In record speed, I remove my dripping fingers and place them between my lips. I was right about her honey. "Sami, you're so fucking sweet."

Quickly I reach for the waistband of her panties, drop to my knees, and pull the little bit of lace down. As I lower it, I find myself eye level with the most beautiful pussy. I spread her legs, showing me her wet thighs, lean forward, and take a deep breath. "You smell as good as you taste."

"Marsh..."

I fight the need to run my tongue through her folds and feast on her sweet essence. However, my tongue has competition. After all, we're in this position because my body has a mind of its own and made no bones about what it wanted.

I want to be inside her more than I want to breathe.

After one quick lick, I stand, our eyes meeting as my tongue goes to my lips. The embarrassment or uncomfortable feeling I always imagined would be there if we went this direction in our relationship is nowhere to be found.

How could it be?

There's no room for that, not with the wild, burning passion.

Fuck, the temperature has quadrupled.

The blaze is out of control.

Sami leans back, her shoulders against the wall, and smiles at me.

I've always known she was beautiful, but I never saw her like this. Her green eyes shine with desire. Her lips are pink and puffy from our kiss. And her nipples are deep red.

She has a great smile, confident and sexy. As one of her hands roams down her tight stomach toward her pussy, she says, "Hurry up, Marshal, or I'm going to do this myself."

My grin twitches. "Bossy. You've always been bossy."

The way her eyes twinkle with just the right amount

of mischief makes my chest expand. I love seeing this side of her. I'll take it over her earlier tears any day.

In seconds my jeans are unbuttoned, and I hurriedly push my pants down to my calves. I want them off, but damn it, my shoes are still on. I'm sure as hell not taking the time to take it all off.

Lowering my boxer briefs, my dick springs outward.

Sami gasps as I grasp its girth. Slowly and methodically, my hand moves up and down as I stroke my huge cock.

I'm not bragging.

It's big.

And with each pump my balls grow tighter and heavier, filling with the need to be inside her. The skin covering my dick is stretched to the max. The shaft is lined with angry veins and the tip glistens.

Sami's eyes widen. "We're even," she purrs, "because you've been hiding that monster cock from me."

Monster.

I grin at her description. "You always did like monster movies."

"They make me scream."

"Oh, I plan to make you scream."

She giggles as I lift her against the wall.

For the first time, I don't reach for a condom. I justify my decision in a split second, knowing I'm clean and my best friend is on birth control.

Sami's as light as a feather. Her toned legs wrap

around my waist, and I line myself up with her entrance. "Once we do—"

Sami reaches down, grabs ahold of my dick, and drops her body. In less than a second, we become one. Her sweet yelp echoes through my apartment, followed by my deep groan as her forehead drops to my shoulder.

"Oh my God, I'm so full."

"Fuck, Sami."

She's so wet I slide inside, stretching her as her heels dig into my ass, and she wiggles to accommodate my size. Once she's completely surrounding me, Sami lifts her head and our eyes meet. "Shut up, Marshal, and take me."

I don't hold back.

I can't.

Being inside her skin to skin is like slipping on a satin glove—one that's two sizes too small. She's so tight. I'm consumed with the need to move, to feel her, and to embrace the friction as her sexy body pounds into the wall and her heels dig into my backside.

Like a wild animal I thrust, deeper and deeper, until I'm as far as I can go.

Over and over I move.

Perspiration covers my skin.

It's as if I'm out of control, and I love every second of it. I don't want it to ever end. I never want to stop, but all too soon, I feel her body clench. With each quiver, she tightens more and more around me. Hell, the glove shrunk. It's now three sizes—four sizes—too small.

It's the best damn feeling in the world, and then all at once, she screams and her fingernails pierce my shoulders.

There are words, but I can't make them out.

Her entire body convulses as wave after wave of orgasm tears through her. She's my best friend and I'm ripping her to pieces and I can't stop. I ride the wave, never slowing for her orgasm, in and out, and then it happens.

My grip on her ass tightens as I pull her closer.

With a roar, I come undone.

CHAPTER
Twelve

Sami

I awake in Marshal's arms.

That isn't a totally accurate statement.

As I regain consciousness, I'm entangled in Marshal Michaels. His muscular arm is draped over my shoulder, and his leg is bent over mine. He is the cocoon, and I'm the butterfly encased safely inside.

For a few minutes, I don't move.

It feels too good, too perfect.

Not only the warmth of his skin and the aroma of our sex-filled night, but everything. I'm in the arms of the one man who knows me better than anyone else in the world, and it's better than any fattening food, alcohol, or drug.

Being with him is perfect in more ways than I want to admit.

Lying in Marshal's embrace, I have the realization that even with Jack, I held back.

Not intentionally, not maliciously, but more out of

self-preservation. I couldn't tell Jack everything. I never told him about my first time.

I couldn't tell him about Todd, who was not only fast but clumsy. I never mentioned my disastrous first attempt at sex. How it hurt or how it lasted about ten seconds. It isn't a part of me I wanted him to know, but it is different with Marshal. He already knows. He knew the day after it happened.

Closing my eyes, I see him the way he looked ten years ago.

It was the day after prom.

While I probably should answer Todd's texts, I leave my phone at home and walk down to Marshal's house. I don't knock. That is the way we are in our neighborhood—one family. When Marshal's mom, Monica, sees me, she smiles and asks if I enjoyed prom.

Nodding, I embellish my answer. I could do that with her but not with Marshal.

As soon as my friend appears at the bottom of the stairs and sees me, he reaches for my hand, tells his mom we are leaving, and tugs me outside.

We don't say a word as we get in his truck.

He stares out the windshield as if he knows what I'm going to say. The sounds of the road amplify as we drive out of our neighborhood. I'm not sure where we are going, and I don't care.

I am with my best friend.

Finally, we pass through the rusty old posts where the gate used to be, at the lake.

With voices near the water, he takes my hand and we walk into the wooded area, our shoes crunching the underbrush. It isn't until we make it to the edge of a recently planted cornfield that we stop. Marshal sits on the grass with his knees bent and his elbows resting on top before he plucks a long piece of grass from the ground and plops it in his mouth.

His silence is wearing on me as much as my uneasiness at what I'd done.

It is as if my skin is stretched and itchy, not allowing me to sit. Instead, I cross my arms over my breasts and use the toe of my shoe to dig into the soft ground.

As the long grass dangles from his lips, such as a 1940s movie star's cigarette, Marshal finally speaks. "You did it with Todd, didn't you?"

I won't lie to Marshal. I never have. My answer is barely above a whisper. "I guess."

His lean body stiffens and his bicep pulses. "I'm going to kick his ass."

I stand straighter as my voice returns. "Why? It's not like you haven't done it with...well, everyone."

"But I'm a guy. It's what guys do. I swear if he runs off his fucking mouth about you, it'll be the last damn thing he ever does."

I scoff. "He won't. Plus, if he runs off his mouth, he's a lying piece of shit."

I like Todd, but I also know how guys can be. I know how Marshal can be.

My best friend's gaze leaves the field as he stands and reaches for my arms. As he stares into my eyes, he asks, "Are you okay?"

I shrug. "Yeah, I'm fine. Not much can happen in ten seconds."

His expression of anger morphs into a smile growing bigger by the second. It's contagious and soon I'm smiling too.

"Ha," he says. His eyes narrow. "Are you serious?"

I nod. With the tension floating away in the spring breeze, I sit next to where Marshal had been sitting and look out at the baby corn.

"Well, that's good to know," Marshal says, taking a seat beside me. "I guarantee that when I let him know that I know that little bit of information, it'll keep him from talking trash about you."

"Little is right." Marshal's smile encourages me to continue with my heart growing lighter by the second. "I mean, I don't have a lot to compare it to, but yeah, little is about right."

I wasn't even that honest with my girlfriends, but with Marshal it has always been easy.

Even now.

With Marshal, it isn't a matter of telling him about my past. I don't have to. He knows it all.

As I lie in Marshal's arms, in his bed, and with his steady breathing in my ear, I force my thoughts to go to my ex-fiancé. I'm still upset about Jack.

And hurt.

And mad.

And surprisingly calm.

It's as if a weight I didn't realize I was carrying is gone.

There's no doubt that the thought of telling my parents the wedding is off fills me with dread; however, I'm also shocked to realize that having that complete thought, coming to terms with canceling the wedding, leaves me relieved.

There is still shock and pain—I think that's normal —but there's also liberation.

I'm not sure if this feeling of freedom will last, but while it's within me, I decide to savor it, to lie in Marshal's cocoon and enjoy the liberty.

Maybe I was rushing the whole marriage thing.

Maybe I'm not ready for that.

Those thoughts and more move in and out of my mind as I finally ease myself from Marshal's bed.

He's still sound asleep, his broad bare chest moving with his breaths.

I hold back a giggle. He should be asleep for a week after last night.

Holy shit!

I never knew a guy could keep going on and on like that. And I never knew that I could come more than once, more than twice—shit, somewhere around five, I lost count.

Over the years, I've listened to Marshal's stories of sexual expertise. It isn't that I thought he was lying. I just figured he'd embellished—exaggerated.

Stifling a groan as I take a few steps and feeling the fantastic stiffness in my legs and tenderness in my core, I make a mental note never to doubt him again. And...I add sexual stamina to my list of things Marshal Michaels has never lied to me about.

After cleaning myself and getting dressed, I check one more time on Marshal. He needs to get up for work, but it's still early, only a little after six. After what he did last night, he deserves to sleep until his alarm rings.

Quietly, I grab my phone and purse and leave him be.

For only a moment, I consider giving him a goodbye kiss, but I don't. After all, he's my best friend, not my lover nor my fiancé. I'll let him sleep.

In the car, I finally turn on my phone.

Fifteen voicemails and thirty-seven text messages. All but one from Jack.

The other voicemail is from my mother.

One message is what normal people leave.

Fourteen voicemails and thirty-seven text messages isn't normal.

It's pathetic.

Without listening or reading, I hit the call button.

Jack's groggy voice answers. "Samantha, what the fuck?"

"Really, Jack? I walk in on you and Ellen, and you're asking me *what the fuck*? You were with her, in our condo, in the bed we share. You were so busy that you didn't even notice I was there."

"Samantha, listen, it's all a mistake. I love you."

"Get out."

"Excuse me?" he asks.

"Get the hell out of the condo. I need to get ready for work, and I don't want to see you."

"No, we need to talk. Where did you spend the night? I've been worried."

Asshole.

He wasn't worried about me when he was busy screwing that slut.

My neck stiffens as I hold back the tears. The sadness and hurt I felt earlier are now replaced by anger, and I'm embracing it. "It's none of your business where I was. You forfeited the right to be worried. Get out of the condo. Don't make me call the police. If I do, I'll have you dragged out of there. Do you want your clients to see that on the morning news?"

"Samantha, you're blowing this out of proportion. I don't give a shit about her. I love you. We're getting married."

"That's where you're wrong. I left the ring for a reason. Take it with you. You have fifteen minutes. Whatever is left of your shit will be available on eBay in a day or two." I disconnect the call. As I do, I realize that my hands are shaking. It's not grief. The trembling is exhilarating, similar to the rush of adrenaline after running a race.

I don't really plan to put his shit on eBay. Hell no,

that would take too much work. The dumpster will be sufficient.

Twenty minutes later, after getting a giant coffee in the drive-thru, I open the door to my condo. An overwhelming scent of flowers fills my lungs. Bringing my hand to my nose, I stand in disgust at the room filled with roses. All different colors. Red. Yellow. White. Lavender.

They're everywhere.

How did he do this, get so many flowers this early in the morning?

And then the answer hits me. Jack saw the ring. He thought I'd be home last night.

"Well, guess what, asshole, I didn't come home."

My nose tickles and my eyes water.

"He's pathetic," I say to the empty condo before sneezing.

I shake my head as I move from room to room. If he were there, I'd throw one of the bouquets in his disgusting face.

He's not.

However, there is a note on the bed.

Samantha,
   My love. I'm very sorry...

                    .   .   .

I don't continue to read or even bother to crumple the paper.

Jack isn't worth the energy. Instead, I drop the piece of paper in a wastebasket, strip out of my clothes, and get ready for a shower. As I do, I recall Marshal helping me out of my panties last night.

His hands, long fingers, and monster cock...

The memories wobble my knees.

I reach for the bedside stand to steady myself, but as I do, I brush my arm against another bouquet. "Ouch." Damn thorns. "Shit," I mutter.

A thin trail of blood oozes down my arm. The small puncture makes me grin.

If I needed any more proof that Jack is a prick, I now have it.

CHAPTER
Thirteen

Marshal

I can't believe she left without a word.

When I woke, Sami was gone, and I never heard her leave.

Normally, I'm fine with waking alone. It's much easier than the *sure, I'll give you a call* speech, but this is different. This is Sami.

I have so many questions.

How is she?

Did she go back to that asshole?

Has she told her parents?

Are we still friends?

The questions run circles through my mind, nearly making me dizzy as I shower and get ready for work.

When I finally give her a call, it goes directly to voicemail. I imagine that she's turned off her phone or at least the ringer.

Did she see him?

The thought alone causes me to ball my hands into fists.

Why does it bother me so much?

Sami was engaged to the asshole.

Why now does the idea of her spending even five minutes with him upset me?

I know the answer.

My rage has nothing to do with the fact that we slept together. It's because he upset her.

By nearly noon, I can't take it anymore. Sami works less than ten minutes from my office, and I have to see with my own eyes that she's all right.

The advertising firm where she works has a front office with a receptionist, Marcy. She's a friend of Sami's and recognizes me as soon as I enter.

"Marshal, are you here for Sami, too?"

"Too?"

"I have no idea what's happening, but she's had, roughly, fifty deliveries. I know it's not her birthday. But she's not spilling the beans." Marcy comes around the desk, steps closer, and flashes me a sexy grin. "Come on, you know everything about her. I bet you know what's happening."

Marcy's one of those people who loves to get the dirt on everyone. She's pretty good at keeping the secret, but she hates being out of the loop.

I adopt my most innocent face and raise my hands. "Clueless. I just came to ask her out to lunch."

"Do you think stuffy Jack won't like her having lunch with other men after they're official?"

My chest aches at the thought of her being official with him, but I ignore it as I keep up my normal routine. "You know me, Marcy, I'm not just an *other* man: I'm Marshal." I lower my voice. "And between you and me, I don't give a shit what he thinks anyway."

She winks. "That's right, you're the man."

I shoot her a wink seconds before I enter the main doors and make my way back toward Sami's cubicle. As I turn the corner, I enter a jungle complete with a chorus of sneezes and sniffles. Maybe it's piped jungle noises like they have at Planet Hollywood. I'm waiting for an elephant to raise his trunk and trumpet.

By the way, I am literal with the description *jungle*.

Not as in, *work is a jungle and only the strongest survive.*

Sami's cubicle is literally a jungle.

Marcy was right. I have to wonder if there were literally fifty individual deliveries, or if one giant truck would have been easier. There's no open space. Even the hallway is lined on either side. The flowers and balloons have oozed out of her area to other spaces around her. Flowers are everywhere I turn, vases and planters, roses and lilies, daisies and irises.

"Achoo." Three rapid sneezes followed by yet another one echo from a nearby cubicle.

"Sami?" I call, looking into the sea of flowers.

"Achoo."

I follow the sound until I find her. When she turns,

she's shaking her head. She has a tissue in her hand, her eyes are red, and her nose is running.

"Marshal? What are you doing here?" she asks as she dabs her eyes.

"I wanted...are you all right?"

She nods as an exasperated smile raises her cheeks. "I told you that I was allergic...achoo!"

A chorus of sneezes comes from around the room. Apparently, she isn't the only one who's allergic.

"What the hell?"

"I know, right?" Sami says. "My condo is full too."

I reach for her hand and give it a tug. "How about getting out of here for some lunch?"

"Throw in some Benadryl and you've got a deal."

I snicker as we make our way out to my car.

"It's not funny," she says with a welcome glint to her green eyes.

"It is. It's also pathetic. Have you talked to him or your parents?"

"Jack. We spoke briefly. I told him to get out of my condo. He did. He wasn't there when I got home, but there were—"

"Let me guess, flowers?"

"Oh my God. I never want to see another flower again as long as I live." She rolls down the window as we start to drive away. "Fresh air. I need fresh air."

Like a puppy on its first drive, Sami leans her face out the window, allowing the breeze to blow her hair back. I can hardly keep my eyes on the road. Considering she just emerged from an unwanted tropical nursery, she looks happy and carefree.

How can that be?

"Sami?"

She can't hear me. When she doesn't answer, I tap the button on the window to raise it just a little.

"Hey," she yells as she pulls her head back into the car. "Are you trying to chop off my head?"

"No, I'm trying to get your attention."

Sami smiles. "You definitely had it last night."

Okay, that's good. She brought it up. Her bringing it up is good.

Right?

"Yeah, about that..."

She reaches over and covers my hand with hers. "As far as I'm concerned, we're still friends. How about you?"

I sit taller. "Still friends, and you were right, by the way."

"I was? About what?"

I turn my hand over so our palms meet and give her hand a squeeze. "Honey, you're a great lay."

Sami shakes her head as pink fills her cheeks. "You know, I'm not sad. I should be. I know my parents will be furious, but for lack of a better word, I'm relieved."

"Good. You should be. You were right about something else. You deserve better than that asshole."

"I do."

Sitting in the deli, Sami takes a drink of her sweet tea and leans across the table toward me. Unconsciously, I catch a glimpse of her tits from the neckline of her blouse.

"Eyes up here, *friend*," she says with a glint to her green orbs, emphasizing the last word.

Reluctantly, I lift my gaze. "I don't know how I've never really paid attention." I lower my voice to a whisper. "They're fucking awesome."

"Well, I could say the same about your monster cock." A cute hue of pink comes to her cheeks. "But I don't want to give you a bigger head than you already have."

I shrug. "It wouldn't be any different than the millions of other testimonials. I could pull them up for you on my website if you'd like."

"You're so bad."

I pull out my phone. "No, I'm serious. Let me show you."

Sami laughs. "You're a jerk and you already showed me everything in real life. I don't need to see the website, thank you very much."

I tilt my head to the side. "Yes, that's what they all say. Every one of the testimonials is a thank-you. A few are engraved."

"I could give you some flowers." She shrugs. "I seem to have a lot of them."

"I'll pass."

Suddenly, she sits taller. "I'm going to go to my parents' house tonight to tell them in person that the wedding is off. I think they deserve to hear it straight from me. I'm afraid it's not going to go well."

"Would you like some company?"

"Seriously?" Her tone lightens.

If I wasn't before, I am now. "Seriously," I confirm.

Sami

*B*ack at my condo, after carting all the flowers down to the dumpster, I change out of the slacks and blouse I wore to work and into a pair of jeans, the kind that already had holes when I bought them. Just as I pull the bright green concert tank top over my head, a knock comes from my condo door. I'd told Marshal to meet me here before we went to see my parents. I'm not sure why I like the idea of having him with me to tell my parents, but I do. It is as if when he offered, another weight was taken from my shoulders.

Another knock.

"Just a minute," I call out as I get closer.

Sliding back the deadbolt, I open the door. Instead of baby-blue eyes and light brown hair, all atop of a kick-ass body, I'm met with darker hair, dark brown eyes, and a so-so body. All right, an okay body.

My gaze meets Jack's. "Leave," I say, placing my hand on my hip.

"Samantha," Jack says as he glances over my shoulder

into the living room of the condominium we shared a mere twenty-four hours ago.

"I'm not talking to you, ever."

"Where are the flowers I left you? Did you get the ones I sent to your work?"

"Just stop, Jack. I almost had to go to the emergency room from anaphylactic shock from so many flowers."

"Then maybe you'll like this better?" he asks as he pulls my ring from the pocket of his sports jacket. It wouldn't kill him to wear jeans and a t-shirt, but he rarely does.

My skin itches with irritation as I cross my arms over my breasts. "No."

"You can't throw us away. Not now. Not so close to our wedding. We have plans and people traveling. People who made reservations. You can't ruin it for everyone."

"*She* didn't, asshole."

My scowl turns to a smile at the sound of Marshal's voice.

Jack turns, coming nearly chest to chest with Marshal, who too has changed from work clothes into something more comfortable. I take a moment to appreciate the way his biceps flex under the tight Under Armour material of his shirt.

"This isn't any of your business, Michaels," Jack says. "Get lost."

I step back and before Jack realizes what happens,

Marshal is inside, leaving Jack still on the outside looking in.

"Obviously," Marshal says, "Sami disagrees."

Jack's jaw tightens. "You know, I allowed the friendship thing between the two of you, but don't put your nose where it doesn't belong. Samantha is my fiancée."

"You *allowed*," I repeat his word. "Well, I have news for you. I didn't need nor do I appreciate your permission. You sure as shit didn't ask for mine before you screwed your intern, and as for the title of fiancée, that's no longer accurate. And one more thing, *I* didn't ruin anything. *You* did. You're the reason the wedding's off."

I look up at Marshal.

My heart flutters as he runs his hand through his hair and shines one of his cockiest grins.

Flutters.

Really?

It's like I'm fifteen again, and I'm just seeing my best friend for the whole package that he is. And boy oh boy, what a package.

"Really, man," Marshal says, "thanks."

Jack shakes his head. "What? Why are you thanking me?"

"For showing your true colors. For helping Sami see the light."

Jack pulls his gaze away from Marshal and brings it back to me. He scans my body. "Change into something appropriate and we'll go to dinner. We can work this out."

I look down at my green concert tank top and holey jeans. "I like what I'm wearing and" —I lift my left hand — "what I'm not wearing."

"Samantha."

His tone is one that says he isn't happy. I stand taller. "Can't."

"Why not?"

Marshal's arm encircles my waist. "She has plans."

"Samantha Ann," Jack repeats, using my full name like I'm a child being reprimanded.

I lean toward Marshal and shrug. "You heard him, plans."

Just then Jack pulls his phone from his pocket and grins. "I just received this text message from your mom. She's asking what time *we'll* be there. She said you aren't answering your phone."

Shit. I plugged my phone in and haven't unmuted it.

"*We* aren't going to my mom's," I correct. "Besides you don't like going there. And after they know the truth, you'll never be welcome there again."

Jack shrugs. "I can slum it for an evening for my future wife."

How did I not see what a presumptuous, arrogant asshole he is?

"If you insist," he says, "we can drive separately." He

looks me up and down and scoffs. "Your outfit is fine for Johnson."

I clench my teeth as he turns and walks away. Stiffening my neck, I turn to Marshal. "Gah, and I was going to marry that asshole."

Wrapping his arms around me, Marshal pulls me close. "What's that guy's problem? He doesn't seem to understand the obvious."

"I'm tired of taking his shit. How about I dish it, for a change?"

Marshal's blue eyes twinkle. "What do you have in mind?"

"Are you up for taking one for the team?"

He raises his brow. "I've always been a team player."

"My parents will be devastated at the cancellation of the wedding either way," I explain, "but if they think I'm happy with the decision and that it was my decision, based on me, not on Jack screwing everything up...I know them. They'll be happy for me. They've always supported me and my decisions."

Marshal's hands lower to my behind, and he pulls me closer until our hips collide. "So are you saying that we go to your parents and tell them about us?"

I nod.

"Then we come back here and I get another one *for the team*?" His eyebrows dance in a way that makes my insides clench.

Damn, I need to change.

With just the thought of his inference, my panties dampen.

"The team," I say, "got many last night."

Marshal takes one step toward me and then another, moving me backward. Once again, I'm pinned between the wall and his hard body. Leaning forward, his elbow lands casually near my cheek and his chin rests on his fist. The spicy, masculine scent of him fills my senses as his blue eyes drink me in. I can't help but think about last night, about his monster cock, and about how having him right here erases all the hurt that Jack's wandering inflicted.

"I want more," he says, his cool spearmint breath tickling my nose.

I try to swallow. "More?"

His grin inches upward, lopsided and sexy as hell. "Our new agreement needs some revision. I don't think we can be friends with benefits if I haven't tasted your pussy."

"You—"

He touches his finger to my lips. "Correction. Not tasted. Eaten, devoured, consumed. That small sample last night has been lingering in my thoughts. Today at lunch, with you right across the table, I kept thinking about it. All day really. Your come on my fingers was sweeter than honey. Sami, I have never told you, but I have this condition that can be serious—life-threatening even—if not treated."

I can't look away even with all of the bullshit in his tone.

"It's a real thing," he says. "You can look it up on WebMD. It has to do with my blood sugar. I need come —sweet and honey-like—to survive. I've searched and searched. Up until last night, my life expectancy was dropping by the day. But now that I found it, I need more."

A giggle bubbles in my throat. "That does sound serious."

"It is." He shakes his head. "The quest has been tireless, but finally it's paid off."

"With me."

"Right in front of me the whole time." The glint in his eyes is sexy and fun. "My life is now literally in your hands." He lowers his gaze and brings it back up. "Okay, not your hands."

"I wouldn't want you to die, not yet."

"I'm much too young. Besides, I have a plan, a plan that could quite possibly save my life." He reaches down and cups my core, then one of his strong fingers begins running along the seam of my jeans, and I wish I would've worn a dress, a skirt, shorts, something. With his other hand he pulls me against him. My breasts smash against his wall of a chest. "My plan will require a regular routine involving my mouth and your life-saving pussy."

My nipples harden as my core clenches at nothing. I try to breathe, but each breath is shallow.

Marshal tucks a piece of my hair behind my ear. "Think about that," he says, "while we're talking to Paul and Jean. Think about my face buried in your pretty pink pussy. Think about your sweet come dripping from my chin as your legs squeeze my face and you shout my name."

My mouth dries and I can't help but wonder if it weren't for him pressed against me, I might fall, my legs no longer seeming capable of holding my weight.

He kisses my lips, sweet and chaste like a friend, but his words aren't friendly. They're sexy and deep. They go beyond my ears to my core, twisting it, soaking my panties, and creating a void I need filled. The ripples of his tone send vibrations deep inside of me as I imagine everything he's said.

His face between my legs.

His tongue teasing my clit and the sight of him dripping with my essence.

I reach up to his scruffy cheeks and pull him closer, smashing our lips together as my tongue invades his warm mouth. Spearmint. I savor the minty coolness as our tongues probe and stroke.

When we finally pull apart, my lips are bruised and his cock is hard against my stomach.

Marshal kisses my nose. "Yes, now we're ready to convince Paul and Jean."

CHAPTER
Fifteen

Marshal

've known Paul and Jean most of my life. I've known all of Sami's family, including her brother, Byron, and her two sisters, Jane and Millie. When we were all children, our entire neighborhood had an open-door policy. Her parents were like my parents and vice versa. Not just hers but all the families in the neighborhood.

Now as we drive to Johnson, not too far from Grand Rapids, a million childhood memories fill my thoughts. A million adventures. A million childish schemes...and in so many of them, the woman sitting beside me was an integral part. I steal a glance her way.

Sami's looking out the window, her lips pressed together in a straight line as she takes in the old neighborhood, the small houses that long ago seemed big and the park where we used to play.

Jack is an ass.

This is hardly *slumming it*.

This is our heritage.

My parents lived down the street from Sami's family for years before they moved to a different neighborhood. Sami's parents still live in the same house where they raised their four children. Though these homes aren't mansions, the houses have fared well, many with new paint, new porches, and all with well-kept lawns.

Driving these streets is coming home.

I reach over and squeeze Sami's hand. "What are you thinking about?"

Her green eyes twinkle. "Your monster cock."

"I don't believe you."

"And why not?"

"Because you weren't smiling. If you were thinking about my cock, you'd be smiling ear to ear." I wink. "Or touching your own pussy."

Sami giggles. "Pretty confident in yourself, aren't you?"

"Yes. See, now you're smiling. Now you're thinking about my cock. If you want me to pull over, I'll be glad to touch your pussy for you."

"Maybe later," she says, not fully dashing my hopes but not raising them any higher.

I try again. "What were you thinking about before?"

"Jack."

Well, fuck. There goes that conversation. "No wonder you weren't smiling."

"I don't want my parents to know what he did. It's not to protect him—it's to protect me."

"You? You didn't do anything wrong."

Her lip disappears as she turns back to the window. "I didn't, but to be honest, I now see that he wasn't my Mr. Forever. I should have realized that. I shouldn't have let it get this far. I should have broken it off...

"I am remembering things, times...I didn't say anything or I just pacified him."

"Pacified?" My grip of the steering wheel tightens. "Tell me he has an anger problem and ever hurt you. I swear to God, he won't live to see tomorrow."

Sami flashes me a grin. "Not like that. He hurt me by cheating. By pacifying I mean that I agreed to the fancy restaurants when I really wanted a burger from The Suds."

"The Suds," I repeat with a grin. "You know, we could go there after we leave your parents. They still bring the food to the window of the car." It is a drive-in restaurant about a mile away that never read the memo that the 1950s are a thing of the past.

"Right now, I don't really feel like eating."

"I do." I wiggle my eyebrows.

Sami reaches over and pushes my arm.

"Ow." I fake pain. "Maybe I should ask Jack if you were violent to him." As soon as his name escapes my lips, I know I made a mistake. It's as if I'd hit a switch and Sami's smile is gone.

She sighs. "He wasn't my forever. If he was that special someone, he wouldn't have tried to make me into someone different, and he sure as hell wouldn't have cheated on me. I didn't see what was right before me. I missed the signs...just to be married. I'm as guilty as he is. And now my parents have to pay the price."

"Sami, I'll do whatever you want. Although, for the record, protecting that asshole isn't high on my list." I squeeze her knee. "Protecting you—I'll do that."

And then we turn the corner and see it.

"Shit," Sami mumbles.

She's right.

Shit.

Fuck.

What the fuck?

In her parents' driveway is a small black BMW. It sticks out like a sore thumb in this neighborhood, and there's no doubt to whom it belongs.

I pull along the side of the street and lean over the gearshift. "Sami, go with it. You want this to be you, to be your decision, then we'll make it about you. That asshole won't know what hit him."

She nods, but her eyes are wide open.

Doubt, uncertainty...they're all staring back at me in a kaleidoscope of greens.

Those aren't the emotions I want to see.

I want passion and laughter.

I want confidence and attitude.

I want to take Jackson Carmichael down, and Lord help us, it's going to happen in her parents' living room.

"Are you with me?" I ask.

"Yes."

I barely hear her.

"Louder."

"What?"

We're still in my car, and I raise my voice. "Say it louder. Say it like you mean it."

Her lips twitch. It's something we used to say when we were young. "I'm with you."

"One more time."

"I'm with you!"

"Damn straight."

I walk around the car, but my Sami already has the door open. I reach for her hand. "Come on, honey." I lean closer. "I'm going to call you that because your pussy tastes like honey."

Sami's eyes blink closed for a little too long. "Marsh..."

I wink. "Come on, honey. Let's get this done. I have a craving for honey for dessert."

She shakes her head as we start walking toward her parents' house. But as she does, her lips are turned upward in a grin. It's not just her mouth but her eyes too.

Perfect.

My Sami isn't the broken ex-fiancée walking into this gathering.

However, the asshole inside will be broken when he walks out.

CHAPTER
Sixteen

Sami

As soon as we step inside my parents' house, I look expectantly past the living room through the archway to the kitchen—to where I know my mom will be. I find her, but she's not alone. Jack is with her. They both turn toward the sound of the closing door. Jack's gaze immediately moves from my face to where Marshal is holding my hand. By his surprised and shocked expression, he hasn't come clean with my parents. At the same time, my mom looks up from the computer desk screen and smiles. Her smile dims as she too sees our hands.

My dad's right in front of us in the living room. However, his focus is on the television. He barely notices as Marshal and I walk through. If we hadn't walked in front of the screen, he might not have seen us.

"Hi, Dad," I say after bending down and giving him a kiss on the head.

"Sami." His eyes leave the television long enough to notice Marshal. Either he doesn't notice our intertwined hands or he doesn't care. "Marshal, how are you? How're your folks? It's been too long since we've seen George and Monica."

"They're good. I'll tell them you said hi."

Dad nods and points to the television. "Can you believe this? They're going to vote her off the island. I just know it. One challenge and they're throwing her out. I think Ralph, the guy with the bandana" —he points to the large screen— "should go. He's a conniving bastard." Before we can reply, Dad pounds the arm of his chair. "No! No! Don't do it."

I pull Marshal's hand, tugging him toward the kitchen and saving him from my dad's tirade.

"Samantha. Oh, Marshal," my mom says, "what a surprise to see you."

"Yes, what a surprise," Jack says in a deadpan tone, his gaze flicking back and forth to our still-connected hands.

Taking a breath, I let go of Marshal's hand and begin speaking, "Mom, Jack, we need to talk about the wedding."

"We are," Jack says.

"Look at this," Mom says, pointing at the screen. "The RSVPs are starting to come in." She looks down at the notebook in front of her where she's written all the names.

"Mom, you know that you can print that list from the program."

"Oh, this is easier. Here just look," she says, handing me the notebook.

Writing each name isn't easier, but now isn't the time to try to convince her of that.

"No. It wasn't her fault. It was that asshole Ralph."

We all turn toward the living room at my dad's outburst.

"Mom, about the wedding..." I try again.

"Samantha, let's go out back and talk," Jack suggests.

"No," I answer curtly.

"Samantha Ann" —my mom narrows her eyes at me as she stands— "what's going on?"

I put down the notebook without reading the names and steel my shoulders. "Like I said, we need to talk." I turn back to Jack. "You shouldn't have come here."

"Samantha, I love you. I'll be anywhere you are."

Marshal, who'd been leaning against the wall, steps forward. "In the future that may be a little awkward."

Jack snaps his head toward Marshal. "Again, Michaels, none of your business. Tell us why you're here?"

"Damn it! They did it." Dad rushes into the kitchen and reaches for the refrigerator handle. "Now I don't know who'll be next."

"Paul," Mom says, grabbing his arm and stopping his progress. "Stay in here. Sami has something we need to talk about."

"No, she doesn't," Jack says.

Marshal takes another step toward me and puts his arm around my waist. "Yes, she does. Or I will."

Mom takes a step back and covers her lips with her hand. "W-what is happening?"

"The wedding is off," I say.

"No, Samantha, don't do this." Jack's tone is as pathetic as his flowers.

I narrow my gaze at Jack.

He speaks over the television coming from the other room. "I was keeping it a secret, but our honeymoon...a villa in the South of France is—"

"Jack," I interrupt. "I don't need a villa or France. I don't need fancy restaurants and a big house in the suburbs in the right neighborhood with the right median income."

He takes a step toward me. "It's what I want to give you."

I shake my head. "No. It's what you want. *I* don't want any of it." I fight tears of frustration. "You want me to be someone I'm not. Little by little, you've been chipping away—"

"Sami," Mom says, reaching out for my hand, "maybe it seems like too much right now—"

"I want to make all your dreams come true," Jack says.

By screwing someone in my bed? I don't say that. Instead, I straighten my shoulders and opt for a warning. "Jack, continue to talk and so will I. I'll say more. Right now,

I'm going with *I'm the one who saw the light. I'm the one who is calling the wedding off.* But I can easily change my story."

Dad nods with his lips together. "Okay." He smiles. "The wedding is off." He turns to Mom. "I'll let the boys know I'm free for golf." He turns back to me. "Is there anything else you need to tell us?"

Turning toward him, I question what I just heard. "Aren't you upset?"

"Not as upset as I am about Missy. I think that Ralph asshole is going to try to get rid of her next. I need to see the end of the show."

"Paul, wait," Mom says, stopping Dad's retreat.

Jack reaches for my hand. Equally as quick, I shake my head and pull my hand back. At the same time, Marshal tugs me closer.

"Jean," Marshal says, breaking the awkward tug-of-war. His tone even gets my dad's attention. "We need to be honest with you. Sami and I...we decided—"

"What the hell?" Jack asks.

"You're free, Jack," I say. "Go screw whoever you'd like." I look up at my best friend and smile. "Marshal and I have decided to see what's beyond friendship."

"You're what?" His face reddens with the realization of what Marshal and I are saying. "When? How long?"

"It's relatively new. But" —I grin Marshal's way— "the best foundation for love is friendship." I turn back to Jack. "And well, you and I...we were never friends. I'm not even sure I like you, Jack. I thought I could love you, but that isn't the same."

"Wait," Mom asks, "you're serious? This isn't just last-minute jitters?"

I turn to face my mom. "I'm saying I can't go through with the wedding. I'm sorry I didn't see this sooner, but, Mom, the wedding is off."

Mom staggers backward until she collapses in a chair.

Dad brushes his hands together. "Well, there we go." He turns to Jack and extends his hand. "Goodbye, Jack. Don't let the door hit you in the ass on your way out." He turns back to us. "If that's all settled, I'm going to finish my show. Missy needs me. That damn Ralph..." His words trail away as he shakes his head, opens the refrigerator, and grabs a beer.

Marshal grins at me and mouths, *I told you.*

"You two are lying," Jack says. "Samantha isn't interested in you" —his noses scrunches— "like that."

Marshal scoffs. "You don't want the details, but let me say...damn" —he turns to me— "if that was you *not* being interested, I can't wait to find out how great we can be when you're interested."

I feel the warmth as my cheeks undoubtedly growing redder by the second. "No, that was me *very* interested."

Marshal turns back to Jack. "I thought you were supposed to be some clever attorney. Tell us, was the ring on the kitchen counter not enough of a clue?"

Shaking his head, Jack looks at me. "Samantha, you're just saying this to get back at me. Fine. I deserve it, but there's nothing..." He motions between me and Marshal. "I've seen you two together. There's nothing more than friendship. Unless you've been lying all along."

"I didn't lie, Jack. I don't lie. Up until very recently, Marshal and I were only friends." I smile at Marshal. "Best friends." I look back at Jack. "That's changed."

"No, Samantha, I don't believe you. Why are you doing this?"

I stand straighter. "It's not because of what you think, but that did give me a chance to re-evaluate."

Marshal turns toward me, his blue eyes a blend of emotions that I'm not sure I can identify. Without words he cups my cheek and kisses me, strong and possessive. My eyes close as I melt toward his chest. By the time I open my eyes, Jack is gone. Seconds later the front door slams.

"Good riddance," Dad says over the sound of the television.

"Dad?"

"What?" he calls from the living room. "I'm talking about the show. They're finally wising up. Ralph's going to get what's coming to him."

I go to my mom and kneel before her. "Mom, I'm sorry."

She shakes her head. "I'm not. I'm really not." She

squeezes my hand and looks up at Marshal. "Is this...real?"

Just then, Dad enters and slaps Marshal on the shoulder. "I don't give a rat's ass."

We all turn.

"What?" I ask.

"We never liked Jack. He's a pompous ass who always acted like he was better than everyone else. I get that he has money, but no one's better than my little girl, and no one needs to make her anything she isn't." He flashes me a wink. "If you ask me, Sami girl, you're perfect." He turns to Marshal and offers him his hand to shake. "Marshal, son, whether you're here as Sami's cover or if there truly is something happening between the two of you, I don't care. If it helped to get rid of Mr. Jackson Carmichael, well, son, the beers are on me."

I look closely at my father's expression. The wrinkles and age I'd been noticing seem to fade away. "Are you sure? What about the money?"

Dad shrugs. "We'll figure it out. If we have to throw a celebration party to announce you're a free woman, we'll do it."

Marshal squeezes my hand.

"Mom?" I ask.

"Paul, get me one of those beers."

CHAPTER
Seventeen

Marshal

After we each finish a beer and Paul makes sure that Missy is safe on the island for another week, I take Sami's hand. "How about a walk around the old neighborhood?"

A grin and a nod are all she offers. Ever since her parents surprised her with their response, she's been quieter than usual.

Outside, the sun has set, leaving the sky dark, the streetlights the only illumination. They project glowing circles lining the familiar street. "Look," I say, "Mrs. Jefferson has a new dog."

We both wave to her.

Mrs. Jefferson waves back, but when she squints, she shouts, "Marshal Michaels, is that you? And Samantha? What in the world?"

She pulls her puppy's leash down the short driveway. He obviously hasn't gotten the hang of walking on a leash as he runs this way and that. She looks at our hands clasped together and straightens her neck.

"Samantha Ann, I thought you were marrying the fancy lawyer guy?"

"Hello, Mrs. Jefferson," Sami says. "The wedding is off."

Mrs. Jefferson studies us for a moment, her gaze again going to our entwined hands. When she looks up at me, she purses her lips. "You could do worse, young man."

I squeeze Sami's hand, well aware that we're still in the friend zone even if we've added benefits. But as Sami smiles up at me, for one of the first times, I wish she were up for a new agreement. "I'm well aware."

"You two aren't getting any younger," Mrs. Jefferson says. "I remember when the pair of you were running around this neighborhood. I always knew you were up to no good." She winks. "That may have been a bad thing when you were ten. But now I bet the two of you have some better ideas on how to cause trouble." She smiles. "The good kind." Her painted-on eyebrows wiggle.

Sami shakes her head, and I see a hint of pink fill her cheeks.

Letting go of my hand, she tries to change the subject. In a second, she's down on her knees. My mind goes to a totally inappropriate place, imagining her on her knees, her sexy tits showing as she takes my dick between her lips. As I work to concentrate on the present, Sami offers her hand to the small brown puppy.

"What's his name?" she asks.

"LS," Mrs. Jefferson answers.

"LS?"

"Little shit," Mrs. Jefferson replies matter-of-factly. "The little shit shits all over the kitchen floor."

Sami grins as she stands. "He sure is cute."

"That's why he's still here," she says, eyeing me and then Sami. "Cute and dependable. I can count on him to leave me his gifts. Cute and dependable. Two very good qualities."

"See you later, Mrs. Jefferson," I say, reaching again for Sami's hand and tugging her back toward the sidewalk.

Once we're out of earshot, I affirm Mrs. Jefferson's advice. "I like cute and dependable, but when you add gorgeous tits and a great lay, I'm even more intrigued."

Sami's tits rise and fall with my words. I can't help but wonder if she would be willing to make a new agreement. But before I can find the right way to bring it up, she says, "It's a good thing neither of us shit on the kitchen floor. Now where are we going? Or are we just giving my parents some time to realize what happened?"

"I'm confident that your dad fully comprehends. Besides, by now he's lost in *Dawn of the Zombie Apocalypse*. He watches those episodes on demand."

"Or he could be rewatching an old episode of *The Walking Dead*."

"Hasn't he seen every episode nearly fifty times?"

She shrugs. "Can't say for sure, but I'd guess the answer is yes."

"Do you remember the old boathouse at the park?" I ask.

Her cheeks rise at the memories. "I do. I remember sneaking in there and smoking your dad's cigarettes. I also remember being scared to death my mom would smell the smoke."

"Do you think they still leave it unlocked?"

Her green eyes widen. "Why? What do you have in mind?"

"Mrs. Jefferson said we were always up to no good. If that boathouse is unlocked, I can be *up* in no time." He brushes his arm against mine. "And this time it will definitely be good. But if things go as I'm thinking, it won't be smoke your mom can smell. It'll be honey."

Her breathing shallows.

"You know," Sami says, "Jane always told me there were monsters in the boathouse, and I needed to stay away."

"Your sister is partially right," I say, leaning closer to her ear though there's no one around as I scan the park. "My *monster* cock will be there in your tight pussy. But I also disagree. You shouldn't stay away."

Sami giggles as we sneak past the closed gate and run through the shadows, just as we did when we were kids. The difference now is that unlike when we were kids, this time my blood is finding a different route of circulation. I'm growing harder with each step and each stealth move behind a rock, bush, or tree.

"Do you think there's anyone in there this late at night?" she asks.

"Probably some kids smoking cigarettes."

"Great, so we'll smell like smoke and..."

"Sex and honey," I say. "Definitely more like sex."

CHAPTER
Eighteen

Sami

We descend the old stone stairs. They're steep and partially covered with overgrown grass and vines. For a moment I wonder if the city has demolished the old boathouse. There's no doubt that it wouldn't make the cut with today's building codes. My sandals slip and Marshal turns and steadies me.

His strong hand secures my waist. "Are you okay?"

In the darkness, I can't see the blue of his eyes, but in his familiar concerned tone I hear both my friend and a new additional protectiveness.

"Yes. I'm good."

We reach the top of the boathouse. It's concrete and built into the hill near the river's edge. Together we tiptoe down the stairs to the front. Pebbles on the shore shift under my shoes. The old metal door is slightly ajar.

"Hello?" Marshal says in a deep whisper.

My heartbeat quickens as we await a response.

What if there are kids?

What about a homeless person?

What about someone more dangerous?

Why does this suddenly seem like a stupid move?

We're adults.

Marshal has an apartment.

I have my condo.

It doesn't make sense that we both have our own homes, and we're sneaking into a seventy-year-old abandoned building to have sex.

Marshal pushes the door. It barely moves, but the squeak of the metal on the concrete is deafening. Using his broad shoulder, he pushes harder. The loud scraping noise sounds like an alarm alerting anyone within a mile of our whereabouts.

With a flashlight app on his phone, Marshal shines a light inside the old building. It appears as abandoned as it was when we were young. Cobwebs drape from the metal beams, in the corners, and over the painted windows. My pulse is thumping like it would at the fair in one of those fake haunted houses.

I cling to his hand. "Do you think there are animals?"

His flashlight scans the floor. "Nothing bigger than a mouse or a squirrel."

"A mouse?"

He pulls me through the partially open doorway. With his phone flashlight off and only moonlight for illumination, the room comes into focus. On the one wall is a tool bench or at least I think it used to be. It's a wooden shelf, about three feet wide, attached to one of the walls. Behind it is a board peppered with holes, similar to one my father has that contains hooks and tools. Marshal brushes the surface and confirms that there's nothing on the bench that breathes.

Then in one quick move, he grasps my waist and lifts me to the bench. My feet dangle as I stop worrying more about mice and bugs and focus on his deliberate movements.

"You were so strong, Sami, facing that asshole." One by one, he removes my sandals.

His words encourage me as he lifts my tank top over my head.

"I wanted to take you right then and there."

He unlatches my bra, laying it on top of my shirt.

"God, I love these tits..." Marshal's words fade as he leans forward and sucks one of my nipples into his mouth.

Both of my nipples bead as he cups my breasts and continues sucking one and then the other. I lean back, holding myself on my arms, longing to pull him closer. "Marshal..."

"I'm going to eat you, Sami."

My insides twist as my pussy clenches. "I thought we were planning that for later at my condo."

He touches my lips. "Did that sound like I was asking your permission?"

Oh shit...

My core twists tighter at his change in tenor. This isn't the tone of my lifelong friend. This is the Marshal Michaels of lore, the one others have talked about.

"Marshal..."

He reaches for the button on my jeans, expertly snaps it open, and peels down the zipper. Leaning forward, he brushes his nose near my core and inhales, the sound filling the old building.

"Lift your ass, Sami, I have honey to eat."

My arms quiver as I do what he says. My jeans and panties move down and soon join my bra and shirt in a pile. Marshal grins as he lifts my feet to the edge of the bench. With my knees high, he pushes them apart, exposing my most private parts.

"You're fucking gorgeous," he says as he scans my exposed sex.

The modest part of me is glad the lighting is dim, but as my core clenches and I grow wetter, there's no doubt that I'm less embarrassed and more aroused.

I gasp as Marshal's tongue swipes my core.

"Hmmm."

I close my eyes as he teases my clit. I'm not sure exactly what he's doing, only that his attention in one area is setting off nerve endings elsewhere and in all directions throughout my body. My scalp tingles, my skin covers in goose bumps, and my nipples harden to diamonds. Marshal is a starving man and I'm his feast.

My arms give out as I fall to my back.

"Fuck, Marshal…" I moan.

His speed increases as my hips jump.

Undeterred, Marshal holds my hips down as he licks and nips. I've never been so consumed. I mean that literally, but also figuratively. The world outside these old walls is gone. Hell, even within these walls. I can't fathom anything or anyone other than Marshal and what he's doing to me.

No amount of wiggling or thrashing will lessen his ministrations. I can't fight his hold, and I don't want to. Yet it's too much stimulation as tiny tremors morph to seismic earthquakes, pushing me closer and closer to my orgasm. It's when Marshal adds his skilled fingers, plunging deep inside me that I scream his name.

"Marshal."

My entire body convulses, flooding my system with the sense of euphoria. It's as my mind clears that I realize that his touch has moved, circling and teasing the place I've never considered allowing anyone to go.

"Marshal, I've never…"

"Shhh, honey, let me show you how good you can feel."

On the few occasions when anyone has tried to breach my tight muscles, I've stopped them. Jack never tried, but with each passing tease, it's apparently clear that Marshal isn't waiting for me to grant him consent.

Of course, I haven't refused him either.

The word *no* is on the tip of my tongue as my breathing quickens.

I bite my lip, losing myself to his touch, confident he'd stop if I told him and equally curious if I don't. The exhilaration of the haunted house is back. Thank goodness, I have my best friend with me, the man I know I can trust.

As his finger pushes past the tight muscles, my back arches and my hips quiver. The stimulation is more than I ever imagined. He's working me with both his fingers and his mouth. Perspiration moistens my skin. Breathing seems overrated as I pant and gasp.

All I can think about is how good it feels, and how I don't want him to stop.

When his thumb strokes my clit, every muscle in my body tightens and wave after wave washes through me. The sound of the river outside is lost as convulsions overtake my body and my feet slip from the bench. By the time my eyes open, Marshal is moving my feet to the floor and turning me around. My breasts are against the old bench, and I suck in a deep breath as his erection pushes against my entrance.

I taste my own essence as he cranes my neck backward and kisses me.

As his tongue dances with mine and my back arches, his monster cock plunges inside me. As it moves in and out, my breasts rub the bench and my core stretches as Marshal works to get his full length within me.

Full.

Deliciously filled.

Marshal Michaels fills me like no one ever has. In no time, my core again clenches as he pushes me toward another orgasm. His rhythm grows faster as his cock continues to harden and grow inside of me.

Again, his finger enters territory where only he's gone.

"Oh...oh...God..." Words are difficult to form.

"That's it, honey. Tonight my finger, but soon you'll have my dick."

I shake my head, telling him no, but the words won't form. I trust this man. I trust my friend not to hurt me. Those thoughts come and go as my body again detonates. My core clenches and hugs his cock. My shoulders fall to the bench and the boathouse fills with Marshal's guttural growl.

The deep rumble reverberates in the concrete boathouse as he throbs within me. Finally, Marshal collapses over my back. We're still connected, his chest covering my back, warming and protecting me.

"I...I...That was amazing," Marshal whispers near my ear.

What was he going to say?

When he doesn't say more...I agree, "It was."

CHAPTER
Nineteen

Sami

I wipe ketchup from my chin as I set the partially eaten cheeseburger in the plastic basket lined with crinkly paper that's sitting upon my lap. With the windows of Marshal's car open and the summer breeze, the scene reminds me a bit of when we were young.

"I don't remember the last time I ate here," I say, looking up at the sign *THE SUDS*.

"Do you remember riding our bikes here?"

"I do." I look over at Marshal, wondering what will happen to us and to our friendship. A wave of sadness washes over me. "Hey, you're not eating your fries."

His sexy blue eyes turn to me. "You see, I had this fantastic pussy right before saying goodbye to your parents." He leans his head back on the headrest. "You know, I've known Jean and Paul most of my life, and I swear they knew what we'd just done."

"I'm a grown-up."

"You certainly are."

I set the plastic basket on the middle console and turn in the seat, pulling my leg up. "Jack would never let anyone eat in his car. He wouldn't even valet park."

"I'm sure there are plenty of things stick-up-his-ass Jack wouldn't do."

I shrug. "Not with me. I'm not sure what he did with—"

Marshal reaches out and touches his finger to my lips. "Remember our rule about details?"

I nod against his finger.

"When it comes to your pussy and" —his eyes roam the neck of my tank top— "gorgeous tits, if it's all the same to you, I'd rather think about them at my disposal rather than at Jack's."

"As long as you don't tell me the next time you screw a stranger."

"Hey, I don't screw strangers. I'm a gentleman. I learn names and sometimes exchange phone numbers."

"Can we do this?" I ask.

"I fucking hope so." His voice lowers an octave. "You, Samantha Ann, are a fantastic lay, but more importantly, you're my best friend. You have been that person to me forever and I always want you to be."

"So our new agreement stands—friends with benefits."

"Best friends with benefits for always."

He pushes the basket toward me. "Eat, honey."

I stare down at the basket. There is at least half the burger and most of the fries left.

Marshal reaches for my chin and lifts my eyes to his. "What are you thinking?"

"I've been dieting and working out for the wed—this thing I had on my calendar."

Marshal reaches for my knee. "Will you take some advice from a friend?"

"My best friend, always."

"Do you like the burger?"

"Oh my God, it's heaven."

"Then eat it and if you're worried about gaining weight, I have a vigorous workout I'd be happy to show you."

Lifting the burger to my lips, I take a big bite. Once I swallow, I smile at my friend. "I think I should take your advice because if the workout is anything like last night, I'll need energy."

"You better eat it all."

After our five-star dining at The Suds, my mind fills with all the times Marshal and I have been there for one another, the stories and adventures we've shared as well as laughter and tears. I reach over and lay my hand on his arm. "Thank you."

"For my cock? You already did at lunch."

I shake my head. "For being you and for being there when I told my parents. I'm a bit surprised at their reaction. And perplexed."

"Perplexed?"

"It seems like everyone saw Jack differently than I saw him. How did I not see what everyone else saw?"

"You're asking that of a man who has known you most of our lives and just realized what a fucking fantastic rack you have." He took in a deep breath. "That doesn't make me the most observant person in this car."

I turn toward the window.

Marshal's words fill the silence. "I think sometimes we see what we want to see."

I look back with a grin. "And you didn't want to see my breasts?"

He squeezes my knee. "Self-preservation." His million-dollar smile shines my way. "You have a wicked right hook."

Music fills the car and seeps from the open windows as Marshal drives us back to my place, away from Johnson and into Grand Rapids. Traffic increases as the scenery changes from fields, trees, and starry skies to stoplights and taller buildings.

Once we get to my condo, Marshal walks with me to the door.

"Does this feel awkward?" I ask.

He shakes his head. "No, Sami. It feels right, natural, comfortable, and fucking exhilarating all at the same time."

Nodding, I open the door. As I reach for the light switch and flick it up, I'm face-to-face with Jack.

The next few seconds blur as Marshal steps in front of me and Jack takes a step back.

"Get out," I say, holding the door open. "And leave your key."

"Fuck," Jack says, sidestepping Marshal. "I didn't think Michaels would be here."

"I'm here," Marshal says, puffing his chest. "You heard Sami, get out." He extends his hand, palm up. "And give me the fucking key."

"Samantha," Jack says, ignoring the wall of a man in front of him. "I'm sorry. I made a mistake, but that's all it was."

"Your mistake has a name, Jack," I say. "Ellen is her name. I recognized her. She works at your firm. You introduced us at the dinner with the head partner at The Rooftop. Were you fucking her then?"

"No."

My hand goes to my hip. "Tell me, is fucking interns part of the program your firm offers? I haven't looked at the website. Is it spelled out or is that clause only in the fine print."

"Samantha, stop. It's not like that."

I point to our—no, my—bedroom. "You screwed her in our bed."

"Tell me what you want. I'll do it."

My lips purse as if I've tasted something sour.

"You're pathetic. The flowers were pathetic." I shake my head. "I was so stupid."

"Sami," Marshal says, his voice supportive.

"No, Marshal, I was. I didn't see Jack for who he is because I didn't want to." I spin toward my ex-fiancé. "Now I see what a pathetic excuse of a person you are"—I shake my head—"and I can't unsee."

"Samantha," Jackson says, "I'm sorry."

"Don't be. I absolve you of your guilt. I actually want to do as Marshal did and thank you. Thank you for showing me your true colors before it was too late." Stretching out my arms, I spin around. "I can't tell you how liberating it feels."

"It will never happen again."

My gaze narrows. "You're right. It won't happen to me because we're done. Thank you, Jackson. Now, for the last time, get the hell out of my place." I see Marshal in my peripheral vision. "Or I'll let Marshal do what he has offered."

Jackson takes a step back. "Touch me, Michaels, and I'll sue."

"Jail time for a friend," he says with a grin.

For a second, I recall offering to torch a house in Lansing.

Reaching in his pocket, Jack takes out a keychain, removes the condo key, and sets it on the table near the door. "Goodbye, Samantha."

"It's Sami," I say.

Without another word, he steps through the door-frame and closes the door behind him.

Marshal gently reaches for my shoulders. "I know I keep asking you, but tell me, are you all right?"

"I will be after I have the locks changed and a new bed delivered."

"Where are you going to sleep?"

I lift my eyes to his and shrug. "The couch, unless you have a better idea."

"How about a sleepover at my place?"

"Let me pack a bag. Tomorrow I'll call the maintenance office about new locks. Oh, and remind me to call the fire department."

Marshal's eyebrows knit together. "The fire department, why?"

"I'm burning the bed."

"There's my girl. How about I get the matches?"

"Partners forever," I say as I go to the bedroom and begin to fill a bag with clothes and cosmetics for work in the morning.

When I turn, Marshal is leaning against the door-jamb with his arms crossed over his wide chest. There is something in his expression that I can't exactly read.

"Now what are you thinking?" I ask.

"I'm sizing up your bed. Fire is a little drastic, but I have a saw." He lifts a hand to me.

My hand seems smaller than before as I lay it in his.

His fingers close and he tugs me to him.

I come to a stop as my breasts collide with his chest.

Marshal's lips come to my forehead. "It's been a long time since I've had a sleepover."

"Last night," I remind him.

"That one wasn't planned. What do friends do at a sleepover? Watch movies. Oh, should we stop for popcorn?"

I tilt my head. "Do you have a movie in mind?"

"No," he says as he cups my behind, tugging me closer. "I can't think of one title at the moment."

"Are you still hungry?" I ask with a grin, my mind going to all he's eaten.

"Not for popcorn."

"Then I guess we don't need to stop."

CHAPTER
Twenty

Sami

"Either spill or set me up with your friend Marshal."

I look up from my computer, lost in the advertising proposal I was putting together for a big athletics company. I like my campaign and feel like it should be well received. I've constructed it all on my own, but I was currently double-checking those of other companies, making certain what I came up with isn't already out there.

Sometimes what seems like unique ideas could have been subconsciously planted by observing other advertising. The last thing my firm wants is a lawsuit claiming copyright or trademark infringement.

"Sorry," I say to Linda. "What?"

She hands me a cup of coffee. I recognize the white cup. It's from the corner shop. As she does, she grins and lifts her shoulders innocently. "Something's up," she says. "I can sense it. Last Friday it was a million flowers and you were distracted. Today you're on cloud nine.

And you're focused, but every now and then you just smile. Is it Jack? What did he do?"

I take a deep breath. "Um, no. It's not Jack."

"What's not Jack?" Marcy asks as she appears around the corner of the cubicle.

A pang of guilt hits me. "I should have told you first thing this morning. I canceled the wedding."

Linda's eyes go wide. "Holy crap. You did what? When were you going to tell us?"

From the neighboring cubicle, Ashley pops her head over the partition. Whenever she does that move, it always reminds me of that neighbor on an old television show my mom used to watch. You never saw the neighbor's whole face. I think his name was Wilson.

"What did I just hear?" Ashley asks. "Damn it, Sami, I already bought your gift."

I shake my head. "I'm sorry. I should have said something first thing. My mom is sending out regrets. It's just..."

"Break time," Linda announces with a clap of her hands.

The clock on the corner of my computer says 9:35. It's hardly time for break. But from experience, I know I'll never get work done if I don't indulge Linda and Ashley for at least a few minutes.

As soon as we all enter the break room, Ashley slams the door and begins her rapid-fire questions.

"What the hell? Details, girl. Now. Was it Jackson? He wasn't as good in bed as you thought?"

Marcy joins in. "I think you tasted a different nectar and decided Jack's wasn't sweet enough."

I square my shoulders. "What?"

"Set me up with Marshal," Linda says, crossing her arms over her chest.

"What?" I ask again.

"It's him. Isn't it?" Marcy asks. Her lips pursed and her brow furrowed, as if she's asking me the most incriminating of questions.

"It wasn't," I answer truthfully.

"*Wasn't?*" Ashley and Marcy repeat together.

"Are you seriously triple-teaming me?" I ask, walking toward the watercooler and pouring myself a cup. I know I have coffee on the table, but I need to move. As the cooler bubbles, I feel all six eyes on my back, waiting, ready to pounce.

I turn around in time to see them eyeing one another.

"Okay," I say. "Promise to keep it quiet. I mean, like, to your graves, never tell a living soul?"

Again, Linda, Marcy, and Ashley look at one another.

"Is it that big of a deal?" Linda asks.

I love her. We've been friends since my first day at the advertising firm. She's refreshingly simple and direct. She says exactly what she's thinking, which, by the way, is a complete contradiction to her work. She's amazing at advertising. She's one of those smart-as-shit people with a naïve personality.

"It kind of is," I say as I sit at the lunch table with my coffee and water in front of me. Taking the lid off the coffee Linda brought me, I blow lightly on the steaming liquid and await their answers.

"Swear," Linda says as she sits.

"Pinky swear," Ashley says as she plops down next to Linda.

"Yes, you can have my firstborn," Marcy volunteers. We all look her way. "What? I mean, when I have a firstborn."

Everyone's focus returns to me.

I take a deep breath and let it all out. "Last Thursday, the night before the flowers all showed up here," I begin, "I went home early and found Jack with someone."

"Like a business thing?" Ashley asks.

Marcy's eyes widen, but she remains silent.

Linda's jaw clenches as she stares my direction. "*With?*"

"With," I confirm with a nod.

"And yet," Marcy says, "I didn't see you on my news-feed for murder."

I shrug. "Had I been thinking clearer..."

"Wait. What?" Ashley asks. "Jack? He what?"

Linda, Marcy, and I continue our conversation. "What did you do?" Marcy asks.

"I freaked the shit out. I left my engagement ring on the counter and called Marshal."

Marcy leans back in her chair and nods. "Sweeter nectar."

I close my eyes, deciding if I should share. Once I close my eyes, my mind is filled with Marshal's words of encouragement: the way he supported me at my parents' house, the way he filled me and surrounded me, the way he's never lied to me, and the way my core clenches at the emptiness that comes after his monster cock pulls out of me.

But...

I know.

Marshal is my friend.

I know I don't want to lose that.

We made our agreement before we were even teenagers. We might have amended our agreement so that we now have benefits, but this situation won't last forever.

This is Marshal Michaels.

He lives in the *right now*.

I refocus on Linda. She may be naïve, but she's also the voice of reason. "...your parents...?"

I shrug again. "It seems as though they never really liked Jack. My dad apparently would have voted him off the island."

Marcy's eyes widen. "What island?"

Linda nods, going on as if Marcy hasn't spoken. "He had an air."

"What does that mean?" I ask, suddenly defensive that neither my friends nor family approved of my ex-fiancé.

"It means...good the hell for you."

I can't help but smile.

"Marshal?" Linda asks. "Are you still willing to hook me up?"

"I don't remember that I ever was. Remember, Marshal and I have a few agreements and understandings. He's not allowed to *date* my friends."

"Hmm," Ashley says. "You called him...?"

"I did. He's been great. Very supportive." I take a sip of the still-hot coffee. "Like he's always been."

"Like, jock-strap supportive?" Marcy asks.

I nearly spit out my coffee and look at her. "Jock strap?"

"Supportive in the *nether regions*," she confirms as she wiggles her eyebrows.

I take a deep breath, trying to hold back my smile. "Maybe."

"Anything more?" Ashley asks.

I shake my head again. "No. Maybe. I don't know. We've been friends forever. That's all it will ever be."

Ashley stands. "Eric and I were friends long before we were lovers. Two kids later, I think there's something to be said about dependability and reliability. Has Marshal always been that person for you?"

"Yes," I reply sheepishly.

"And have you been that for him?"

"Yes."

"Do you love him?"

I don't have to think about my answer. "Yes."

"Like a brother?" Linda asks.

I take a sip of my coffee. "I don't know how to define it anymore."

"I think you can safely answer that you're not setting me up with him," Linda says with a grin. "And here I was willing to give you up for him."

"No, you weren't."

A smile spreads across her face. "Never. I think you should see where this goes."

"I think I want that."

"And I'm not even mad about your present," Ashley says. "I'm going to keep it."

"Well," I say, "I'm getting a new bed. I'm not keeping one where Jack screwed a bimbo."

"Burn that baby," Marcy says.

"That was my first thought."

"Bonfire at Sami's," Linda says.

CHAPTER
Twenty One

Marshal

fter scanning my membership card, I make my way from the front desk toward the treadmills. The gym is filling fast, not unusual for early on Friday morning. As I walk to the locker room, I'm not thinking about the chick with the tits and ass. To be totally honest, my mind is filled with Sami. I woke this past Sunday morning in her apartment and in her new bed. My body was wrapped around hers. She was sound asleep and snoring. Okay, not snoring. She was breathing in rhythm, and it was adorable. The way her lips were parted, my mind went to all sorts of possibilities.

Instead of acting on any of them, I tucked my arm beneath her and pulled her close. The way she cuddled against my chest was everything I never wanted but found instantly lovable.

With each passing day of this amended agreement, I continue questioning my existence.

I'm Marshal Michaels.

I fuck.

I move on.

Never.

Never ever.

Never have I woke, cuddled, and been happy about it. There was this one time in college. I'll blame the alcohol and the fact that the chick was a cheerleader and so flexible...but the point was...I woke...she cuddled.

I got my ass out of Dodge.

Sunday morning, I didn't run. I lingered as the scent of strawberry shampoo tickled my nose and Sami's curves fit perfectly against my planes. As she slept, I didn't move. My dick did...because, well...Sami was there.

Cuddling.

Breathing.

And just there.

Unlike the time in that crazy-small bed in the gross off-campus house, this time Sami didn't have an issue with my morning wood.

Morning sex was nearly as great as nighttime.

Every time with her is off the charts.

In my apartment.

In the boathouse.

At her place.

It is as if in her presence my dick forgets how to be anything but hard.

In the eight days since her discovery of—or awakening to—Jack's true self, we've talked.

That is part of our relationship that hasn't changed. Sami and I have always talked to one another; even when talking to other people was hard to do, we had each other. Changing our agreement hasn't changed that tradition.

She and I talked about her parents, about Jack, and about the cancelled wedding.

Despite—or maybe because of—everything, Sami seems to be in a good place...so I did what friends do. I went home.

That was Sunday afternoon.

Today is Friday, and I'm fucking obsessing.

We've had dinner twice and I've feasted on my favorite honey too, but it's as if I want to know where she is and what she's thinking every second we're apart.

I've never checked my phone every ten minutes.

Until now.

If she wasn't Sami, I'd be calling her.

But this is virgin ground.

The friendship zone.

The benefits zone.

Otherwise referred to as hell.

I step onto the treadmill and hit enter. I go through the steps, entering my age, my weight, and choosing the course I want to run. My fingers push without my thoughts engaging. It isn't until I'm partway through my warm-up that I notice Miss Tits and Ass beside me. Every few steps, she side-glances my way.

You know...not turning her head. Not *really* looking, just eying me with a frown.

I recall my previous plan. Lift my shirt, wipe my brow, claim my friend's distress, but the truth is that I no longer give a shit about her.

The realization is one of those epiphany moments— the proverbial sky opening and a chorus of angels singing.

"Marshal Michaels" —their voices come together in a melody of chords— "isn't noticing a fine piece of ass."

Okay. Angels most likely don't say *ass*.

Nevertheless, it is an epiphany.

I don't care about Miss Tits and Ass.

I don't give a shit whether she is upset or forgives me. Even my body isn't interested.

Maybe I'm broken.

No, it's that after what my body and I have experienced with Sami over the last eight days, all either one of us wants is to go back to her place and...

Stay.

Hibernate.

Fucking cuddle.

I run faster on my treadmill, increasing the incline, and hoping that maybe I'll care about the woman beside me or that my desire will change.

I don't and it doesn't.

I pick up my phone while wiping the sweat from my eyes.

I haven't spoken to Sami since last night. It feels like it's been a year.

I'm Marshal Michaels—chicks call me.

Blinking away the sweat, I squint toward my phone, hoping, praying for...

One message.

One call.

It's all I want.

But there's nothing.

"Marshal? Are you going to explain yourself?" Miss Tits and Ass asks.

For only a split second, my body reminds me of a saying: A bird in the hand is worth two in the bush.

I fight the urge to grin. I'm thinking one in the hand is definitely not worth one in Sami's neatly trimmed bush.

"Sorry," I manage. "We didn't exchange numbers and an emergency came up."

She narrows her eyes as she picks up her pace. Her tits sway as her feet pound the treadmill. "So let me give you my number."

I almost choke on my response. It's new to me, but for the first time I can remember, it's the most honest response I can give. "Thanks. You should keep it. There's someone else who I'm kind of seeing."

Miss Tits and Ass doesn't miss a beat. "If you're only *kind of* seeing someone, I'm free for the part of you that isn't seeing someone." She shrugs. "I'm kind of seeing a few people, too."

When had I ever turned down casual, no-strings-attached sex?

My memory is a little fuzzy from before I turned fifteen, but going out on a limb, I'm going to guess the answer is never.

Smiling, I say, "I'll remember that. Right now, I need to see where this is going." With that, I put my earbuds back into my ears and concentrate on the pounding bass, pushing myself to keep up the pace.

I'm not sure what Miss Tits and Ass says or if she even responds. I'm too busy wondering if I should forget another of my policies and call Sami. As I think and run, and think and run...I recall calling her on Friday morning after our first night together. Maybe I'm already treating her differently.

My thoughts work to justify myself.

Last week, I tell myself, Sami and I were still more squarely in the friend zone. We'd only stepped outside the box one night. A week and a day later, it feels different.

Now with her memory come twinges and recollections...the noises she makes just before she comes. The way her pussy tightens. Her smile as our breathing steadies.

My blood should be pumping as I run. It should be racing through my heart and exiting to all parts of my body. But as I think about her sweet honey, her perfect tits, and the way she says my name, I begin to worry I might get lightheaded.

My blood isn't doing its job. Instead, my dick twitches, hardening with each recollection.

CHAPTER
Twenty Two

Sami

message pops up on my screen from Marcy out at the front desk.

You have a visitor.

I can't stop the smile that spreads over my face as I anticipate sexy blue eyes, a chiseled jaw, a rock-hard body, long muscular legs, all topped with light brown hair that looks even sexier after I've run my fingers through it.

We've been at this new agreement for over two weeks and neither of us seems ready to change it. I haven't seen him since he left my place on Saturday morning. I've thought about him, but I kept reminding myself that while we have benefits, we are friends. Friends don't spend all their time together.

Every time I considered calling or texting yesterday, I refrained. However, now with him here on a Monday at my work, I'm reminded of all the reasons I wanted to reach out.

The clock in the corner of my screen tells me it's a quarter after twelve.

Maybe Marshal wants to go to lunch, or maybe we have time for a quickie in his car.

Warmth fills my cheeks as I leave my desk and work behind, and I briefly entertain the idea of doing it in Marshal's sports car. In all honesty, I'm not sure it's physically possible. After all, he's six feet three, and his car isn't big.

Maybe I could suggest my SUV.

If we lay down the back seat...

My expression blanks as I turn the corner and see not Marshal but my mom. I open the door to the entryway. "Mom. What a surprise."

"I was in the city and thought maybe we could have lunch together."

This is the first time I've been face-to-face with my mom since the showdown in her kitchen. We've spoken on the phone many times, but I haven't seen her. "Of course. There's that sandwich shop down the street that you like," I say. "We could walk." I peer through the glass doors. "It's a nice day."

"That sounds perfect."

"Um, let me grab my phone and purse."

When I come back, Mom and Marcy are deep in conversation. Call me paranoid, but I believe it's about me.

Is it about the cancelled wedding, Jack, or Marshal?

That's the million-dollar question. "Ready?"

Warm air blows my hair as we step onto the sidewalk. As we walk, we chat about nothing in particular. I ask her why she's in Grand Rapids, and she asks me about work. It isn't until we're seated and waiting for our order that her expression changes.

The woman across the table isn't a stranger. I know her better than most, and I can tell that our chance lunch isn't by chance and our conversation is going to get more serious.

"I wanted to talk to you without your dad."

"Why?" My heart beats faster. "Is something wrong? Are you sick? Is it Dad?"

Mom's lips come together in a grin. "No, honey. Nothing like that."

Honey.

I have a flash of memory but push it away. "What did you want to talk about?"

"I've sent all the regrets for the wedding."

The guilt is back, pushing on my chest, making it difficult to breathe. "Mom, I have savings. I make good money. Please let me pay for whatever you can't get back. After all, this is my fault."

She shakes her head and reaches for her purse. At the

same time, our number is called from the counter. I
don't move, waiting for whatever she is about to show
me. "Mom, what is it?"

"Go get our food, and I'll show you."

Each step to and from the counter feels like I'm
dredging through quicksand. I don't know what to
expect, but I know it's not good.

When I set our plates on the table, I see a folded
piece of paper under her hand.

Mom swallows and nods. "I told you we planned for
weddings, for all three of you girls. We did. Yours was
going a bit above—"

"Mom, let me pay."

She shakes her head. "The caterer was fantastic. We
lost our ten percent deposit, but that's all. And the
reception hall had a waiting list. It seems you made
another couple very happy."

I sigh with relief, thinking this is better news than I
anticipated.

"The dress," she goes on, "can't be returned. You
could always choose to wear it...you know, when..."

"I'll pay you for the dress and we can burn it in Dad's
firepit."

"Samantha Ann, it's a beautiful dress. Sharon, you
know from the Moose Lodge, well, she said you could
sell it online. She mentioned eBay and Facebook
Marketplace."

I scrunch my nose. "It feels wrong, like I'd be selling my bad choices to some unsuspecting bride-to-be."

Mom nods. "Really, it was all going well until—" She slides the piece of paper my way.

Neither of us has touched our lunch except for a few sips I've taken of my sweet tea and the few Mom has taken of her lemonade. I look down at the paper and back up.

"Whatever this is, you're saying Dad doesn't know?"

"Not yet. I was..." She nods toward the paper. "Please take a look and we can talk about it."

Slowly, I unfold the paper. It takes a few seconds for the words to register. As their meanings become clear, a new emotion—anger—builds inside me.

"An invoice?" I ask louder than I should. "Jack sent you a damn invoice." No longer am I questioning. I know the answer. It's right in front of me.

"Shh," Mom hushes me.

"Fifteen thousand for the canceled honeymoon. Six thousand for canceled travel and lodging for members of his family. And another five thousand for my wedding ring." Each statement was louder than the last. I shook my head and lowered my voice. "Don't worry about this, Mom. I'll tell him to take this and stick it *up his ass*." Okay, I tone it down for my mother. "...where the sun doesn't shine. And he has the damn rings. I gave him back the engagement ring and he never gave me the wedding ring." I shrug. "The jewelry store had a great return policy on the ring I bought him."

Mom takes a breath and picks up her fork before stabbing a piece of her salad. "You did the right thing, Sami."

"I did the right thing too late."

"No, divorcing that man and possibly fighting over parental rights would have been too late. You made the right decision just in time." She takes a bite of her salad.

My appetite is gone as I look again at the invoice, the one that is typed on letterhead from Jack's law firm. I look back up with new resolve. "He's not getting away with this. You aren't paying him a dime."

"I thought about calling him myself, but he's a lawyer and I already know he doesn't think very highly of me or your father."

Hearing her say that hurts more than if she were saying Jackson hated me.

Mom went on, "I guess I'm afraid he'll talk circles around me and somehow make me feel responsible."

"Mom, I'm so sorry. Don't worry about what Jack thinks. He isn't worth you fretting. And I'm serious about the dress. I saw the price tag and I know the cost of alteration. I'll transfer that amount into your and Dad's account this afternoon." I lean back and stare some more at the invoice. My mind wrestles with my emotions.

I am pissed.

No, I was pissed when I found Jack in our bed with Ellen.

Now, I'm full-out furious.

"What does he think he can do, take you to court?"

"I would assume he thinks we'll pay to keep him quiet."

"What the hell" —I lean forward and lower my voice — "is there for him to say?"

"I don't want to worry your dad, but the only way we could pay what he's asking is to cash out some of our retirement."

"You're not doing that. I'll talk to him."

I look at my phone. After the incident in my condo when he gave me back his key, I blocked his number. I have no idea where he's living. He'd sold his place when he moved in with me. He didn't have a best friend with a place to sleep over unless he was staying with Ellen.

I start to nod.

"What are you thinking?" Mom asks.

"I'm thinking that I blocked Jack's number. I have no idea where he's staying" —a smile came to my lips— "but I know where he works. I know the senior partner and I know..." I wasn't going to go to the subject of Ellen.

Mom wipes her lips with the napkin. "Millie mentioned another woman." She looks at me through her lashes. "Don't be mad at your sister. She thought I knew."

The air leaves my lungs. "I didn't want you to know."

"You were protecting him?"

"No, I was protecting me." I lean closer, lowering my voice. "If Millie told you, then you know I walked in on him and that woman. Doing. It. At. My. Condo."

Mom nods.

"Does Dad know?"

"No. Your father is the gentlest of men except when it comes to—"

"Zombies," I offer.

Mom grins. "His children."

I sit taller.

"I just want to know, Sami, did you call off the wedding because of what he did or because of what you and Marshal did?"

I press my lips together. "I canceled the wedding because when Jack did what he did, it was a slap in the face, a wake-up call. I called Marshal because I needed my friend. As I drove to Marshal's place, I saw my future all play out, Mom. I saw me in a big house, in the right neighborhood, with three kids, and Jack off screwing a secretary, neighbor, housekeeper, or maybe the nanny."

It's cleansing and cathartic to be this open and honest with Mom and with myself.

"I didn't see my forever or my always. I knew that night that Jackson would never be either of those people for me and going through with the wedding would have not given me what I've always wanted." I swallow again, tasting the salty emotions. "He lied about France. I opened an email and saw our honeymoon reservations. They were for New York. We had reservations at a swanky hotel and tickets to shows. I'm sure it would have been great, but it wasn't France.

"He's a liar. That's who he is and who he will always be. I saw the future. I imagined that each time he would cheat that he'd bring me a piece of jewelry or take me somewhere expensive." My head shakes. "That's not how I want to spend my always."

Mom reaches across the table and covers my hand. "Sami, you made the right choice. May I ask...what's happening with Marshal?"

The sadness and frustration disappear at the mention of his name. "He's my always, just maybe not like I dreamed. Marshal is..." —I inhale as I look through the windows to the sidewalk— "like Mrs. Jefferson's dog."

"LS?" Mom asks quizzically.

"He's cute and dependable, but I know him and eventually, he'll shit on the kitchen floor."

Mom's eyebrows knit together. "Remember that book I read you when you were little. You and your sisters and brother used to giggle the whole time." She doesn't wait for me to answer. "*Everyone Poops*."

I chuckle. "I remember that."

"What are you afraid of?"

I give her question some thought. There are too many answers. I could say spiders or mice. I could say having someone cheat on me again. But my greatest fear surpasses all of those things. "Losing my best friend."

Mom smiles. "Are the two of you honest with one another?"

"Always."

"Don't let that end because you've added...benefits."

"Mom." My eyes widen.

"Oh, Sami, I'm old, but I'm not that old. I suspected when you came to the house—after he kissed you. Honey, that was the kind of kiss that melts a girl's panties. It definitely wasn't a friendly peck on the cheek."

Warmth creeps up my neck to my cheeks as I recall the kiss.

"But at that moment, I also wondered if what I was seeing was an act for Jackson's benefit." I start to tell her it wasn't, but she goes on, "And then you returned from your *walk*." She shakes her head as her smile grows. "The two of you looked at Dad and me like you did after I caught you smoking in the old boathouse."

I clear my throat.

"Oh, funny story."

"Tell me," I say, happy for the change of subject.

"Well, it's more like strange." She grins. "That very same night the two of you went for a walk, on the Neighborhood App, someone reported hearing strange noises coming from the boathouse. They called the police, but by the time the police arrived" —she shrugs — "the boathouse was empty."

I reach for my sandwich and bring it toward my lips. "That is strange."

CHAPTER
Twenty Three

Marshal

I stare down in disbelief at the paper Sami has just handed me. When I look up, my gaze meets her beautiful green one. "What a fucking asshole."

She shrugs as she settles on the couch at her place. "We knew that."

When I received the text from her this afternoon asking me to come over, I wasn't expecting a conversation about her ex. I could say I wasn't expecting anything, but that would be a lie. And even now, seeing her wearing soft shorts, a tank top, and I would guess no bra, I could let my mind wander with possibilities. The thing is that I'm Sami's best friend first. The benefits are secondary. Right now, she needs a friend.

As I study her expression, I see the small lines near her downcast eyes. Even after she kicked his ass to the curb, her ex is still a source of her angst. My stomach twists with a memory, and I face the fact that I failed her. "Sami, I'm sorry. I should have said more."

"More about what?"

"That night we were all at the same bar...remember downtown...The Rooftop on the top floor of the Marriott?"

"Yeah. Do you know I walked two blocks in those ridiculous shoes and that short dress just so I wouldn't valet park his precious car?"

I remember the night and the snow beyond the windows. "There had to be six inches of snow on the ground."

"Well," she says, "thankfully, the sidewalks were clear."

I sit next to her and reach out, squeezing her knee. "That night, before you got to the bar—"

"I was probably trekking along a freezing cold sidewalk as salt pellets crunched under my high-heeled shoes."

A grin comes to my lips. "Probably. Can you shut up a second and let me talk?"

Sami's head shakes. "Bossy."

"You like it."

That changes her sad expression to a grin. "Sometimes."

"Anyway, that night, while you were exploring the frigid streets of Grand Rapids in totally inappropriate hiking clothes..."

"And shoes."

I inhale. "...and shoes, I saw Jackson and watched from the other side of the bar."

Her brow furrows. "Watched what?"

"I don't know for sure. And that's why I didn't say anything, but if I went with my gut, he was flirting with the blonde."

"Ugh." Sami stands and paces around her living room. "That blonde is her. That's Ellen." She spins. "She probably isn't a real blonde, but I didn't get close enough to take a look while she was in my bed."

I let that comment pass as I move forward. "I went over to him. I guess I wanted him to know I saw him."

Sami wraps her arms around her torso as her expression clouds.

Standing, I walk to her.

I can't stop myself. It's as if Sami's a fucking magnet, and I'm helpless but to obey the laws of force drawing me to her. I don't stop until I reach out and wrap my arms around her soft slender body and pull her against my chest. The scent of strawberries whiffs through the air as I inhale.

"I was such a stupid idiot." Her words are muffled against my chest.

"No, I should have said something."

Sami leans away and as her gaze meets mine, she slaps my arm. "You should have. Why didn't you?"

"Ow." She couldn't physically hurt me if she tried. Okay, she did when we were five but not now. Now, I'm only crying wolf to see her smile. And it worked.

"That's why," I say as I run the pad of my finger over

her cheek. "Your smile. It lights up a fucking room. I've seen you happy, and I've seen you sad. Never, and I mean never, do I want to be the cause of your sadness. And I think when I saw him with her, I didn't want to say anything, on the off chance I was wrong."

"You, Marshal Michaels, considered the possibility that you could be wrong? Wow."

My expression turns sober. "I wasn't, Sami. I knew that, but I didn't want to be the one to tell you. I saw how controlling he was, and I didn't want you to be put in a position where you had to choose. Maybe I didn't just consider I could be wrong, I considered I could be right and it would cause problems between us. Fuck, I couldn't bear to lose my best friend."

She wraps her arms around my torso and lays her head against my chest. "I don't know what I would have said. It would have hurt coming from you because you're the one person I know has always told me the truth."

I kiss the top of her head. "I'm sorry."

"No. Seeing Jackson for the ass he is was something I had to do. I don't even think you could have gotten through to me."

"I'm still sorry, Sami. He should be fucking dust in your rearview mirror, not still causing you and your parents heartache."

"He lies. He says what he thinks will help him." She sighs. "Remember what he said about the honeymoon, in Mom and Dad's kitchen?"

"France."

Her head shakes. "It wasn't true. He'd booked a week in New York." She looks up at me. "I need ideas, Marsh. Come on, you and I defeated the stormtroopers every night before the sun set. We waged battles on our bicycles against make-believe bad guys." Her emerald stare shines through her lashes. "This time the bad guy is real. He's a prick with a tiny dick who thinks he has the power and that he's better than everyone else. He's taking his embarrassment at my canceling the wedding out on my parents."

"It goes without saying that your parents aren't paying that."

"I'm sure that Jackson knows that legally, he doesn't have a leg to stand on. I know him. He's just trying to get in one last jab."

"Tiny?" I ask.

Sami soft-punches my back. "Focus."

"You said *tiny*."

"I thought we weren't supposed to share details."

"I don't want details on what he did with it, but you could elaborate on your description. Mushroom head? Weird kink or bend? Go on."

Shaking her head, she steps away. "I'm pretty sure that every man in the whole world will seem tiny from now on."

Friends with benefits means we are willing to accept that our friend will most likely move on to someone else.

However, as more seconds tick by, I'm having trouble accepting that fate. While I'm happy to be the new gold standard, I'm not a fan of any other dick—big or tiny—getting near Sami.

Not now.

Not ever.

"What, Marsh? No comeback about how I could add that testimonial to your website?"

"One thing at a time," I say, reaching for her hand. "How do we stop tiny-dick?"

"I've been racking my brain ever since Mom gave me that paper. That's why I called my always-and-forever partner in crime. I mean, if we could defeat make-believe bad guys on the daily, together we can come up with a plan."

This is my Sami, the one who never gives up, who is always thinking. "Let's go get some dinner and keep working on this."

She looks down. "I'm not exactly dressed."

As I scan from her head to her painted toenails, my grin broadens. It's as my gaze lingers on her spectacular tits that her nipples harden, tenting the tank top.

"Jeez, Marsh, stop. You're..." She didn't finish the sentence.

"What? I'm just looking at you."

"Yeah, but your eyes are all molten and simmering."

"I don't even know what that means."

"It means we have a problem to work out, and with

just one look, I want to forget that problem, forget dinner, and go give my new bed another workout."

I tug her hand toward the bedroom. "Okay."

"No. Food, sabotage tiny-dick, and then sex."

"Is the order of operations set or" —I try flashing her one of my famous grins— "is there some wiggle room?" I almost mention that her little itinerary combined with the thought of her wiggling has me hard, but since she shook her head, picked up her purse, and is headed for the door, I think the part of me that's growing harder will have to wait.

"Fine," I say, "You drive a hard bargain."

It isn't until we're nearly halfway through our sushi that something she said earlier hits me. I lay down my chopsticks. "Wait, what did you say earlier about the honeymoon?"

She dips her California roll in soy sauce and looks up at me. "He lied about France. He wouldn't tell me what he had planned. It was supposed to be a surprise. But I accidentally opened an email of his and saw the itinerary. Like I said, he had a week booked in New York."

I cocked my head to the side. "How did you *accidentally* open *his* email?"

Her eyes open wide. "Shit. He programmed his password into my laptop one time when we were on a weekend getaway. His laptop was out in the car and he had to reply to..." She starts nodding and bouncing in her chair. "Oh shit. I have access to his email."

It takes all my self-restraint to keep my eyes on hers and not at the way her free-range tits are bouncing beneath that tank top. "Do you think he's changed the password?"

"If he's smart..." Her smile grows.

"Right."

"Hopefully, he's forgotten that he did it."

Just before I stuff the last roll of sushi in my mouth, I say, "Let's go back to your place and see what we can find."

CHAPTER
Twenty Four

Sami

I'm so excited to find out if we have access to Jackson's emails that I tug on Marshal's hand, hurrying him from the parking lot to my condo. "Hurry."

"I thought you liked it slow," Marshal responds as his long strides catch up with and pass me until he's the one in the lead.

Grinning, I shake my head.

I'm not sure if I never noticed all of Marshal's sexual innuendos, or if I did and they didn't used to affect me. Either way, I love how comfortable we are with one another and how easy it is to be together. There was a part of me that was afraid sex would change things.

Maybe it has changed things.

In a good way.

Once we're in my condo, Marshal follows me to my bedroom.

"Hey, why are we in here?" he asks as his eyebrows

dance. "I know. You've decided that the bed workout comes before taking down tiny-dick?"

"No, there'll be no *coming* before taking down tiny-dick."

Marshal smiles, snaps his fingers, and points to me. "You're good."

"I told you I was." I sit down at my desk and open my laptop.

"Where were you?"

I crane my neck to see Marshal's face. "When? What are you talking about?"

"Where were you when he used your laptop?"

I let out a long sigh. "Holland."

"The country?"

A smile curls my lips. "No, Michigan."

"Whoa, big spender," Marshal says as he sits on the edge of my bed. "Did you fly or take the thirty-minute drive."

As my computer is coming to life, I think back. "It was a spontaneous getaway. And it was tulip time." I smile. "We stayed at this quaint bed-and-breakfast. Actually, we went there on multiple occasions. The couple who owns it is so nice. I think Jackson did some legal work for them."

Marshal lies back on the mattress, his knees bent and feet still on the floor. I can't help but notice the way his blue jeans fit, how as he lifts his hands over his head, his shirt rides up exposing that sexy V that some men have.

Turning back to my computer, I remember what I said earlier, how all men would pale compared to Marshal.

It's not only his monster cock that puts him in a league all by himself.

It's him.

Maybe that's been my problem with finding my forever and always.

I met mine at five years old and have been comparing everyone ever since. I don't think it's been a conscious thing, but as I imagine what he's hiding under his blue jeans and my core clenches, I know the bar has been raised. Before it was Marshal's friendship that was the standard measurement; now it's so much more.

"Here it is," I say, clicking onto Jackson's email account.

Marshal is up and off the bed, his handsome face next to mine as he leans near my shoulder.

"It looks like him."

"What does that mean?" I ask.

"Boring."

I start scrolling, reading each subject line. I have to agree it's not enthralling reading. "What about folders?" I ask as I continue to navigate through Jackson's private information.

There are hundreds.

Who has hundreds of folders?

"Shit," Marshal says, "look at all of those."

"And they're all labeled with initials. It will take

hours to go through them all." I sigh and lean back. "I don't even know what I'm looking for."

Marshal's strong hands come to my shoulders. His long fingers squeeze and massage.

"Oh." I roll my head on my neck. "That feels so good."

"Don't let him make you tense."

I can't see my best friend, but I feel him. It's not only his hands on my shoulders and neck, but it's also his calming presence. "I think in some way, Jackson always did that."

Marshal's hands come off my shoulders. "Well, then I won't."

"No, please don't stop. It feels amazing." Once again, Marshal is behind me, squeezing and massaging. "Yes..."

"What did he do?"

"No details, remember."

"Honey, you're not talking about sex. I know that."

My head shakes as I close my eyes. "Made me tense. I didn't see it as it was happening. Like that night you were talking about, at that bar. I'd spent the day with Mom looking at wedding dresses and I didn't realize that the time for dinner had been changed. I hadn't looked at my texts, so even though I thought I was on time, I wasn't."

Marshal didn't say a word as his fingers continued their magic.

I wasn't seeing the computer screen right before my eyes but rather memories.

"He said it was to help me, but he had that black dress and those shoes laid out for me. You said he was controlling. I didn't see it." I spin in the chair coming face-to-face with Marshal's baby-blue stare. Emotions I've successfully avoided bubble inside me, churning our dinner. "How did that happen?"

Marshal's lips meet mine and I reach out to him, surrounding his thick neck until my breasts are against his solid chest.

When our kiss ends, I shake my head and blink away unwanted tears. "Marshal, you've known me forever. Is that me? Am I so easily manipulated that I would allow someone to control me without my realizing it?"

Taking my hand, he pulls me from the chair onto his lap as he sits again on the edge of the bed. For the longest time, he stares, brushing strands of hair from my face and over my shoulders. Although he isn't speaking, I hear him, his turmoil and his angst. Whether he and I are intimate or only friends, there isn't another soul on this earth who could answer my question with as much knowledge as Marshal.

"Are you," he finally says. It isn't a question but a prelude. Marshal's head shakes as the depth of blue in his orbs swirls with emotions. "No, Samantha Ann Anderson, you are not."

"Then how—"

His finger comes to my lips. "You're fucking strong. You're adventurous. You're smart. You're brave and fucking loyal to your core. You're also incredibly gorgeous, and if I haven't mentioned it before, you have the best rack I've ever seen."

My lips curl as I tip my forehead to his. "I sense a *but*."

His fingers splay beneath the hem of my shirt. "Oh, yeah, you have a fine ass."

"Marsh."

He takes a deep breath while leaving his warm hands against my skin. "No, there's no *but*. There is a sidebar. You saw a future, one you've been wanting since we were kids, and Jack offered that to you. You were so busy seeing the dream that you didn't notice the nightmare lurking off-screen. Are you easily manipulated? There's only one person who can do that to you." He kisses me. "It's you, honey. And the good news is you saw it, you figured it out, and you stopped him. That's what his stupid invoice is to your parents. It's him trying to take back power." He tilts his chin toward my computer. "That over there is you refusing."

"Maybe that" —I lean my head toward the computer— "can wait. I'd really like to forget about him for a while and be reminded what it's like to feel good."

Marshal takes ahold of the hem of my shirt and lifts. There's no resistance from me as he pulls the tank top over my head, drops it on the floor, and stares down at my breasts.

"Hello, ladies." He pulls his gaze away from them and as his blue eyes meet mine, he shakes his head. "No bra, you naughty girl."

Warmth climbs my neck to my cheeks as my skin tingles and my nipples bead. "I wondered if you'd noticed."

"Only the second I walked through your door."

Reaching for his shoulders, I lean close and bring my lips near his ear, knowing I can be honest with him. "No panties either."

"Oh fuck."

His bicep bulges as with one hand, he pulls his t-shirt over his head. Every toned muscle makes itself known in his washboard abs.

"Do you think the research can wait?" I ask.

"I think we can find something better to do."

"You think?"

"No, honey, I know. Lose the shorts."

"So bossy."

"I am, and you like it." He lifted his chin. "Scoot up the bed. I haven't had my dessert yet."

CHAPTER
Twenty Five

Marshal

I wake to that feeling that it's not morning, yet the world is calling. As I blink my eyes, I see the way the otherwise-dark bedroom fills with light and different colors. Reaching for Sami, I find only cool sheets. They weren't cool by the time we finally gave into sleep. No, they were on fucking fire.

Unabashed receptiveness is something I need to add to my growing list of Sami's attributes.

Sitting up, I see my best friend through the darkness, sitting at her desk in front of her laptop. The light from the screen reflects off her white satin robe and her long chestnut hair is now piled on her head in a messy bun, giving me a sexy silhouette of her slender neck as she shakes her head.

I blink again and again, finally noticing but not understanding what she has on the screen.

As I roll to the side, the sheet drapes over my waist and leaning my elbow on the mattress, I prop my head on my fist. "You've been holding out on me."

She flinches at the sound of my voice as she cranes her neck toward me. "How?"

"You never told me that you were into porn."

Her face inclines before she spins the chair toward the bed.

Before I can speak, I'm struck by her expression. No longer is it the blissful one I saw as she cuddled against my side, laying her head on my arm and drifting off to sleep. From the illumination of the screen, I see her anguish. It isn't only visual. Fuck, I feel it vibrating through the air as I scramble from the covers to look closer.

"No," Sami says as she stands, her small frame trying to shield the screen. "Please, Marsh."

I'm fully nude and that fact isn't even on my radar. All I can concentrate on is Sami as I reach for her shoulders. "What the fuck, Sami?"

Letting her chin fall to her chest, she takes a step to the side.

I stare, my eyes glued to the woman on the screen.

Porn isn't new to me.

My education started young, sneaking peeks at Bruce Jefferson's dad's stash of *Playboy* and *Hustler* magazines. He kept them hidden in the attic of their detached garage.

When I was older, Robbie Thompson discovered pay-per-view. Every Friday night I and a few other boys would spend the night. That didn't last long, only until his parents received the detailed billing.

Next, I figured the internet was safe until I learned about a thing called browsing history. That led to an interesting conversation with my mother, one that neither of us wants to remember.

I could blame my viewing on curiosity or even hormones; however, no matter the root cause, as I became older, I found the real flesh-and-blood version far surpassed images or even movies.

I'm hardly a prude. I enjoy a woman's body for the amazing creation it is, and right now, the woman standing and staring up at me is so racked with emotion that it takes me a minute to understand.

I blink my eyes again, certain my mind is playing tricks on me.

Perhaps I'm still in bed and this is some kind of erotic dream.

One more look at Sami confirms that one person's dream is another person's nightmare.

My focus leaves the screen and goes to Sami.

"What the fuck? Did you pose for that? Are there more?"

A tear slides down her cheek as she shakes her head. "There are more. I don't know how many." Her words come out staccato, punctuated by her rapid inhalation.

That fucking prick.

"Did you pose?" I ask.

"No." She wipes her cheek with the back of her hand. "I didn't know."

"Are all the pictures of you?"

"No." Her volume rises. "Oh hell no. Based on quantity alone, I'd say I wasn't his favorite model."

I'll take her raised voice to tears any day of the week. "You have every right to be pissed." I point to the screen. "You're saying he took that picture and others without your consent." I didn't phrase it as a question, yet she answered.

"Yes. Without my consent. Without my knowledge."

Sami spins around and enlarges the picture. Though it becomes very pixilated, I finally figure out what she's showing me, the bed. I turn toward her bed. My memory is fuzzy.

"The bed we got rid of, is that the one in the picture?" I ask.

"No. This was taken in Jackson's place before he moved in with me." She flails her hands as she points toward the screen. "I've been looking at these for over an hour. The majority of them were taken at his place. I'm so damn angry. I think he must have had some kind of camera set up in his bedroom. But look..."

She sits and quickly scrolls. "See this one?"

"I've looked at porn with friends before, Sami, but for the record, this isn't doing it for me."

"Good. Don't look at the woman." She points to the

window. "Look at the trim around the window. See the color. I'm certain I know where it is."

"What does that mean?"

She grunts as she again scrolls. "Don't look at me in this picture. Look at the color of the window casing."

It's fucking hard not to look at her. Damn, she's stunning. Yet what gets my attention isn't her perfect body; it's her face. "Shit, Sami, you didn't know this was being taken?"

"No."

"Why aren't you happy?"

She quickly stands. "Maybe because I just found my ex-fiancé's treasure trove of self-made porn. No, I think it's called revenge porn."

"Only if he puts it out on the internet."

"Well, it violates some law."

"I think it does." I rephrase my question, wanting an answer. "Why aren't you happy in the picture?"

She shakes her head. "God, I was such a dunce."

My blood pressure spikes. "Why aren't you happy in that picture, Sami?" My hands ball into fists at my side. "Did that asshole force you?"

"No." She shakes her head. "If I were to guess— because that's what it will be since I don't remember that exact instance—I would say that we argued and this was about to be make-up..." She shrugs not finishing her sentence. "He has this thing where he likes to watch."

"Watch what?" My mind is a cyclone of thoughts.

Watch Sami with another guy.

Watch her with another woman.

Watch her with herself.

"Sami, watch what?"

She turns away. "No details, remember."

I can't stop myself as I reach for her shoulder and turn her until she's facing me. My question comes out louder and gruffer than I intend. "Watch *what?*"

"Me touching myself." She lifted her chin toward the computer. "Let me rephrase. He likes to watch *women* masturbate. Like I said, I wasn't even his star model."

Fuck.

Holding onto Sami's shoulders again, I gently run my hands up and down the soft satin sleeves. The robe she's wearing is barely long enough to cover her round ass. And if I tug on the sash, I am sure I could get a real-life view of the tits on the screen. Instead, I stay in friend mode. "As long as you were okay with it..."

"I wasn't okay with pictures."

"Tell me where you saw that weird color trim."

"It's not weird. It actually looks nice. Wait..." Her eyes open wide as she pushes past me and picks up her phone on her bedside stand. "Shit, shit," she mumbles, scrolling and looking down at her phone. "I deleted most of the pictures with him in them." She stops and looks up at me. "Here. I must have kept it because his face isn't in it." She shoves the screen my direction.

I see a table near an open window. On the table is a

wine bucket and glasses. It's then I see the same trim. My gaze meets hers. "Where was this?"

"In Holland."

"That bed and breakfast?"

She nods. "It's called Feliena's Room. Jack liked it because it's larger than other rooms and has exclusive access to the porch."

"Apparently," I say, going quickly through the pictures, checking out the ones with the greenish trim, "it also has exclusive access to cameras. I know this is hard, but look at the angle of all of the pictures."

This time, Sami is looking from behind me, her hands on my back as she peeks around my shoulder. "You're right."

"Do you know the identities of the other women?"

"Some," she says as she sits on the edge of the bed. "There are dates. I'm not certain if the dates are representative of when the pictures were taken or when he uploaded them."

Turning away from the screen, I run my fingers through my hair. "I don't understand why he has them in his email."

She shakes her head. "I've been looking through them for a over an hour. I'm not the only woman in pictures with dates after our engagement. Hell, Ellen and I aren't even the only two. It seems that after he sold his apartment, he primarily used the bed and breakfast."

"This can't be legal."

Sami sighs as she falls back on the bed, lifts her arms over her head, and stares up at the ceiling. "You're naked."

It is the first time since I crawled out from the sheets that I even considered it.

"Do you want to take my picture?"

Faster than fast-pitch softball, Sami grabs a pillow and chucks it at me. "No. Don't joke."

I walk toward her, then lean over her and climb onto the bed until I have her straddled. "Listen to me."

With an over six-foot-tall, two hundred-plus-pound naked man straddling her, Sami puts her hands over her ears and starts singing. "La la..."

"Oh no." I reach for her hands one at a time until I have both wrists secured over her head, and her wide-open green eyes staring up at me. "You, Samantha Ann, will listen to me."

"You can't make me."

"I am making you. I have you pinned and your wrists captive." Keeping her hands secure, I do what any naked friend would do. I untie her robe, stare down at her perfect body, and begin tickling her.

Sami tries to resist, but within seconds, the bedroom rings with her laughter as she wiggles and writhes beneath me. "Stop it," she cries between giggles. "I'm going to pee."

Letting go of her wrists, I reach for her waist and roll

until she's on top of me. Somewhere during the tickling, giggling, and rolling, Sami's long hair became loose and is now hanging down around my face, leaving us in our own tunnel.

"Thank you," she says before leaving a kiss on my lips.

"Honey, I'll take your laughter over tears any day."

"I don't know how you do it."

"Do what?" I ask, tucking her hair behind her ear.

"How you can find me angry and sad and make it all go away."

"I wish I could make it all go away, but I think you found the answer to that asinine invoice tiny-dick sent your parents. How about this weekend we take a trip to Holland?"

She nods as my cock remembers that Sami and I are more than friends.

We're friends with benefits, and now that we're awake and unclothed, it's time for more benefits.

CHAPTER
Twenty Six

Sami

"Did you request Feliena's Room?" Marshal asks for the third time during this thirty-minute drive.

"Yes, but on short notice, they couldn't guarantee we'd get it. Honestly, we may not get a room at all. Besides, I've been thinking. How can we prove that we didn't install cameras if we find them?"

"This isn't about legal action against the bed and breakfast. It's about confirming our suspicions."

I stared out the window of Marshal's car as we made our way into Holland. "You know, this is such a cute town. I hate that he has ruined it forever."

Marshal's hand comes down gently on my knee and squeezes. "Only if you let him." As we brake at a stop sign, he looks both ways. "It's been forever since I've been here." He turns his sexy smile my way. "Do you remember coming here for field trips?"

"I do. I think my mom still has wooden shoes with all of our names on them, even Byron."

"With the upturned toe."

"Yes. If I remember, the shoe is made that way so you can walk. The wood doesn't flex, so you kind of roll when you step."

"See," he says, "I told you that you're smart. I'm an architect and I didn't know about wooden shoes."

"You better not make a bid to build the little old lady's house."

Marshal's gaze narrows as he looks my way.

"You know...the little old lady who lived in a shoe."

The car fills with his laughter. The sound washes over me like a warm shower. It's so familiar and yet unexpectedly comfortable. I lay my head against the headrest as we approach the Centennial Inn. "Parking is behind the buildings, off Central Avenue between 12th and 13th."

Marshal slows and turns into the parking lot, and as the tires bump over the joining of two uneven surfaces, my stomach drops. "Stop."

Marshal hits his brakes and we both lunge forward, only to be stopped by our seat belts. "Well, fuck," Marshal says. "Maybe that's not his BMW."

I shake my head. "No. It's his." My eyes go to the second floor of the clinic building. It's the rectangular building behind the main old Victorian home. As I scan the windows, I feel the growing pressure as my heart thumps against my breastbone.

Marshal pulls his car next to Jackson's BMW.

"What do you think you're doing?" I ask. "We're leaving."

"Or we can go up to that room" —his chin lifts toward the clinic building— "and knock on the door, tell him exactly what we know, inform his companion that she's most likely being photographed, and let him know if he so much as sends Paul and Jean a fucking Christmas card, you will take his photo collection to Fred Wilson."

With each of his phrases, my eyes open wider. "Shit, you've thought this out."

"You've said parts of that." He reaches for my hand. "I just put it all together in a nice little concise package for you. But hey, honey, if you have a better blackmail in mind, forget mine and go with your gut."

I inhale as I look up at the building before us. "My gut says run."

"That's not your gut." He lifts my hand to his lips and brushes kisses over my knuckles. "It's not. You are the girl who convinced me to sneak out of my house and walk around the cemetery after midnight. You were the one who took the beer from your refrigerator, and we shared it in the boathouse."

That makes me smile. "The beer was warm and gross. I think I threw it up." I tilt my head. "Now, the more recent memories of the boathouse were your idea."

He extends his hand, palm up. "That's because we're a team."

I lay my hand in his. "Are you sure we can't be a team back at my place or yours?"

"We can be a team anywhere. I suggest we walk around the city, grab some food and drinks, and enjoy Holland because you're not going to let a tiny-dicked asshole ruin this town for you. Besides, I haven't seen the windmill since fifth grade."

I take one more look up at the windows of Feliena's Room. "Fine. This is better anyway. I won't need to go to his office. I can get it over with and move on."

"As long as I'm with you, I'm all for moving on."

My focus moves from the building to Marshal. "I like you with me."

"Convenient. Now, let's go so you can wipe this turd from your wooden shoes."

"You really want to walk around the city and riverfront?"

"I do."

I reach for the door handle. "Follow me."

The thing I know about Marshal is that I never have to ask him twice or wonder if he has my back because he always does. We reach the outside door as a man I don't recognize exits with a nod, allowing us access inside the building without a key.

"That was lucky," I say as we face the staircase to the second floor.

"I had it all planned."

"No, you didn't."

The higher we climb, the more I question my sanity. If this were only about me, I'd walk away and let Jackson enjoy his kink even if it's wrong, but it isn't only about me. I see my mom's face as she showed me the stupid invoice and hear her tone as she fretted about finding the money to pay Jackson.

Cash out their retirement.

Hell no.

By the time we reach the top of the stairs, my shoulders are square and my neck is straight and tall. I turn to the door to room 7, Feliena's Room, and knock.

"Just a minute," a woman's voice calls.

I don't recognize the voice. I look at Marshal as we both shrug.

The doorknob turns and the door moves inward.

Ellen's eyes open wide with recognition.

"Ellen."

She pushes on the door, but Marshal is too fast, blocking the jamb and holding the edge of the door. "Hello," he says. "I believe we met at The Rooftop bar."

"Where is Jack?" I ask.

"He...he..." She resigns herself to the fact that the door won't close as she steps back and wraps her arms around her stomach. "He went to get ice."

"I'm not going to ask," I say, "if we can come in. We are."

"Samantha" —she begins as Marshal and I enter the room— "I don't know what to say."

I turn and face her. Thankfully, she's clothed, wearing a pair of tan slacks and a bright orange halter top with a high neck.

"I understand your dilemma. After all, a speech that includes *I'm sorry I fucked your fiancé in your bed three weeks before your wedding* probably requires some rehearsal. Don't bother."

Marshal taps my arm. When I turn, I follow his line of vision and I see it. If I didn't know better, and when I didn't know better, I thought the object in the corner of the ceiling was a sprinkler head. Now I know better.

"What?" Ellen asks.

"I was going to wait for Jack," I say, lowering my voice, "but there's no harm in you knowing what I didn't." I don't wait for Ellen to respond. "See that sprinkler head?" I point upward. "It's a camera."

Her eyes widen and her lips form an "O."

"Yes, it recently came to my attention that my ex-fiancé has a thing for photographs."

Ellen shakes her head. "I don't believe you."

Marshal shrugs. "I suppose that's your prerogative. I'll just let you know that not all men are a fan of the bald look. Trim it. Tend it. Just give us something that says we're not fucking a child."

I almost added that we still didn't know if she was a true blonde but refrained.

Small noises of shock come from her throat as she takes a step back and the door behind us opens.

"Ellen, I found—" Jackson staggers before his gaze meets mine. "What the fuck are you doing here, Samantha?"

"For the love of God, try saying Sami. It won't kill you."

He reaches for his phone. "Get out. I'll call the police."

"Your..." I turn to Ellen. "What exactly are you? His intern? His fuck toy? His girlfriend?"

"She's my associate and you're no longer anything, so this doesn't concern you."

"I bet it would concern Fred Wilson," Marshal says. "He just happens to be friends with my boss, Jason McMann's father. Shut up and listen to Sami, or Fred and Martha's home will be our next stop."

"This is none of your business, Michaels."

I walk to the desk near the wall and pull out a small tablet embossed with the letterhead of the bed and breakfast along with a pen and hand them to Jackson. "I need you to write a note stating that neither my parents nor I owe you any compensation for any expenses related to our cancelled wedding. And be sure to sign your name." I look to Ellen. "She can sign as a witness."

"Why would I do that?"

I sense Marshal ready to pounce.

Instead, I look Jackson in the eye and relay the message my best friend gave me minutes earlier. "We know about your inclination to photography. We've already informed Ellen, but if you do as I say—write the note and leave my parents the hell alone, and I mean alone as in no contact ever—if you do, we'll leave. However, if you don't comply, I will take the pictures of Ellen and of you and Ellen to Fred Wilson. I doubt that fucking interns is part of the partnership program."

"If you do, I'll make the pictures of you public."

"Go ahead and try," Marshal says. "I did research. Michigan is one of the states with laws against revenge porn."

"Misdemeanor," Jackson says.

"No charge looks good for an attorney," I say, "especially one who recently made partner. And then there's the whole matter of photographing without consent." I turn to Ellen. "I assume you signed a waiver before allowing Jackson to take photos?"

She's standing taller, looking at my ex with venom that I understand. Ellen's gaze narrows. "I have not."

"Hmm," I say. "What about the others, Jack? Do you have consent from *all* of them?" I emphasize the word all.

Marshal is leaning against the wall near one of the windows that is painted with the telltale greenish-blue paint. Before Jackson responds, Marshal speaks, "Sami, do you know all of their identities?"

"No."

"I believe that law enforcement is better equipped to do that. They can do facial scans and—"

"How in the hell did you get your hands on any of the pictures?" Jackson asks.

It seems as though denial is no longer part of his plan. I would hesitate to tell him except I've saved every photo onto a flash drive. I spin around, taking in the room. "One time when we were here, you had to send an email, and instead of going out to the car to get your laptop, you used my computer." I shrug. "You really should be more careful with your passwords."

Jackson takes the paper and the pen and walks to the desk.

We all wait.

Finally, Jackson stands and hands the pen and paper to Ellen.

"Are you serious?" she asks.

"Sign the damn paper."

Once she does, he comes close to me, pushing the paper my direction. "We're done."

As I take the paper, I can't help but laugh.

Before I can say anything, Marshal reaches for my hand and tugs me toward the door. Speaking to me, he says, "You're right, he is quick."

"I was talking about something else, but yes."

"Wait," Ellen calls as Marshal is closing their door.

We stop.

"Could I get a ride back to Grand Rapids?"

"No," we say in unison.

As we step outside into the warm summer air, I lift

my face to the sun and inhale. Marshal's arm comes around me and he pulls me to his chest. "I'm so in awe of you, Sami."

"It feels good, liberating." I lift the sheet of paper. "And my mom will be relieved."

"I heard there's a cute town with a windmill. Would you like to join me?"

"I would."

CHAPTER
Twenty Seven

Marshal

I see Miss Tits and Ass move to the treadmill next to mine. She's hard to miss with her giant XL fake tits squeezed into a top that is probably a size too small. Hell, the way they're bouncing, I'm half expecting them to spill out.

Instead of focusing on her, I concentrate on the music blaring through my earbuds, the increase of the incline on my course, and way the speed is picking up. My mind goes to Sami and the way she handled tiny-dick in Holland last weekend and the look of relief on Jean's face when we went to their house for Sunday dinner.

Damn, Sami was kick-ass.

I know through the years there have been times I wanted to protect her, to save her from assholes like him. A grin comes to my lips as I recall one time in college that I was so certain this arrogant asshole—I can't recall his name—was going to try to get to her, I kept guard all night.

In reality, I slept, but I did it while keeping her beside me.

It was the first time I willingly slept next to a woman. It was also the time I did it with no thoughts of sex on my mind. I was too consumed with kicking the guy's ass if he showed up.

Times have changed.

It would have been easy for me to take care of Jackson the way I handled that guy in college. After I woke to Sami's tears as she looked at his photo collection, I was willing. I'm definitely able. And I'd do jail time for her.

That isn't what she wants or needs.

One of the parts of friendship that can be difficult is not stepping in, not taking care of shit for her, and allowing her to handle it in her own way. Yes, I encouraged her. Yes, I was beside her and ready to be her muscle if needed. And it worked. By simply being at her side, I had a ringside view of her knockout punch.

As we walked around Holland, going to the shops, eating ice cream, and having dinner, I kept watching her, wondering if she would be upset that tiny-dick was with Ellen or about the photographs. She had been, but Saturday afternoon she looked and acted exactly as she said.

She was liberated.

I adore seeing her happy and carefree.

After dinner, we drove west until we reached the

shore of Lake Michigan, and sitting on the light-colored sand, we watched the sun set.

There's no doubt that I'm getting too used to waking next to her. It's not only waking. I'm getting used to the whole package.

Crawling into bed beside her and enticing her to put away the Kindle and concentrate on something a bit more strenuous and much more fulfilling.

After three weeks of off-and-on togetherness, I'm surprised by how fucking ready I am to be inside her. I'd been wrong. Being with the same woman isn't mundane or boring. Hell no. Each time with her there is something new, something better than the time before.

We've been going at this now for nearly three weeks.

That thought reminds me of the date.

Shit.

In two days, it'll be her wedding date.

I scramble to think of something to help her get through that date.

Of course, my first thought is more sex.

I mean, it's a cure-all for what ails you, right?

It always works for me.

But for once, I'm not thinking about me. I'm thinking about her. It's funny how just thinking about Sami reroutes my circulation.

My treadmill begins to slow for my cooldown. I'm twenty-five minutes into my thirty-minute run when a piercing scream shatters my bubble and scatters my thoughts. I turn just in time to see Miss Tits and Ass in mid-air, before landing herself half on the floor and half on the treadmill.

Jumping off my treadmill, I offer her my sweaty hand. "Are you all right?"

She brushes herself off and takes my hand. Her hold lingers as she stands. "I guess you're my hero. You saved me."

I pull the earbuds from my ears, not positive of what she said. I mostly noticed the way her puffy lips moved. It's a revelation I hadn't realized was even possible. With this woman's hand in mine, I see her as I never have.

Don't get me wrong, I'm not judging; I'm assessing.

I'm seeing her bleached blonde hair, Botox-enhanced lips, and fake tits.

Is she pretty?

I suppose.

No matter how pretty she is, she's fake; she's emblematic of all the women I've been involved with. No wonder in the past I haven't wanted anything permanent. The women weren't permanent. They were all similar to this woman, an illusion of what is supposed to be sexy.

"You know," she says, "since you saved my life, I owe you three wishes."

Freeing my hand, I reach for my shirt and wipe the sweat from my eyes. As I do, her gaze goes to my abs.

Shit.

This is my move except it's not.

It's only sweat.

When I don't speak, she says, "I'm still available for drinks."

"I'm still—"

"You said you were *kind of* seeing someone," she interrupts. "It's been a few weeks. Are you still only *kind of?*"

"It's complicated."

She lifts a painted and manicured finger to my chest. "I'm not complicated, Marshal. I know what I like, and I'm a no-strings-attached kind of gal. Tell me that doesn't appeal to you."

It would have.

A month ago, I would have jumped at the chance.

Three weeks ago, I had.

"You seem nice," I say. "The thing is that I need to figure out where this relationship is going."

"I'm here if you make any decisions," she says with a sexy smirk. "Besides, I have to grant you three wishes. It's the life-saving rule."

I come up with a lame excuse and head into the locker room. The entire time I'm showering and getting ready for the office, I think about what she offered and why I'm not interested.

The whole time I am thinking about Sami.

She and I need to talk.

I know we have been talking, as well as doing other

things, but my little confrontation with Miss Tits and Ass makes me realize I'm not satisfied with Sami's and my amended agreement. Sami has just recently earned her freedom, and I don't want to take that away, but damn, I want more.

I've played the field. I know what is waiting on each base.

Well, really *who's on first, what's on second, and I don't know is on third*—that's from one of my dad's favorite Abbot and Costello bits.

In all seriousness, if I don't tell Sami how I feel, I'll never know if there's a chance. If I do tell her, I may lose her as my friend. If I don't, someone else may offer her forever and always.

The back and forth continues.

Once I'm settled behind my desk at my office, I pull out my phone and send a text.

"Hey. We need to talk. Dinner? Pizza, my place or out?"

CHAPTER
Twenty Eight

Marshal

I wait for Sami's text message like a high school kid. Shit, I've never waited for a response even when I was in high school. Not even for her.

Why?

Because back then, I knew she'd eventually respond.

She always did.

Always.

Why the fuck am I nervous about it now?

Did I think she'd really let me down?

I didn't want to think she would.

And then it happens. The simple chime and there it is on my screen.

Text message from Sami:

"Talk? Sounds ominous. Food, though, sounds great. Your place is good. Not pizza. Grill?"

. . .

I don't want her to think ominous.

"Not ominous. See you at six."

* * *

At ten minutes before six, I have my apartment all set.

I stopped at the store on my way home from work.

The steaks are marinating and ready to pop on the grill, charcoal is warming, wine is chilling in the refrigerator with salads, and there are potatoes in the oven. The small table on my balcony is set with two place settings, and there is even a candle in a jar.

It's as I stand half in my apartment and half on the balcony that I realize the pansy I've become.

A candle.

I have a fucking candle on the table.

It wasn't planned. I just saw it. The grocery store had candles on an endcap thing. And the moment I saw it, it seemed like a good idea. That was then.

Now the stupid candle doesn't seem like a good idea.

Now it screams desperate.

Hell, I'm no better than tiny-dick and his roses.

Is Sami allergic to candles?

Fuck!

As I run my hand through my hair, I glance down at

my button-down shirt, the way I have the sleeves rolled, and my jeans hanging loosely from my hips.

How and why am I nervous?

When have I ever been nervous about a woman?

This is Sami, my Sami. We've had dinner together thousands of times.

Shaking my head, I decide I should change into shorts and a t-shirt when a knock on the front door stops me.

I don't even look through the peephole. I know who I want to have on the other side. And damn it, I'm Marshal Michaels. I need to get my shit together. If I want this thing with Sami to be more than what we have with our new agreement, if I want Sami to see me as more than a friend, then I need to act like the man who's been sweeping women off their feet for over ten years.

Not like some lovesick schoolboy.

I take a deep breath and open the door, flashing my biggest and brightest smile. "Sami..."

My lips slam shut. It's not Sami. It's Miss Tits and Ass.

"W-what are you doing here?" I ask.

She takes a step forward, her perfume engulfing me as she shakes her tits, barely encased in some tight, stretchy top. I fight to breathe through the over-whelming stench of sweetness while noticing how the skinny straps of her top dig into her shoulders. Poor things. No little bit of material should be expected to support such huge—and fake—tits.

"It's a matter of survival. I have to repay your kindness or my luck will change. And well, Marshal, if the mountain won't come to Muhammad" —she sticks out her mountain of tits— "then Muhammad must go to the mountain."

"I thought I made it clear at the gym."

One more step and her hands are on my chest. "You said you were *kind of* seeing someone. I'm here now and I see you." Her eyebrows rise. "You can see me." She splays her fingers over my chest. "I want to see more of you."

"No."

Miss Tits and Ass takes a step back. Her expression is that of a wounded puppy, but instantly she's back, her plump lip extended in a pout. "Come on, Marshal. I want you to fuck me. I'm not asking for anything more..."

Just then the door at the bottom of the stairs opens, the one that accesses all the apartments in this unit. The gush of fresh air thankfully whisks away the cloud of perfume.

"Damn, that smells..." Sami's words fade and her feet stop as she approaches the stairs. "Did I have the wrong night?"

Miss Tits and Ass stands taller and scans Sami from head to toe.

Sami is radiant and just as I imagined, completely the opposite of Miss Tits and Ass in her high heels and tight dress. Sami's long hair is pulled back in a ponytail that hangs low on her back. Her sundress is simple yet sexy. I know Sami, and I know that her wearing a dress took as much effort as my wearing the button-up shirt.

It's a good sign.

We're both trying.

And that makes me grin.

"Her?" Miss Tits and Ass asks. "You're choosing her over me?"

Sami doesn't move or speak as she stands a flight of stairs below and watches the scene unfold.

"Sami, come on up," I call. "Yes" —I start to say Miss Tits and Ass's name, but I can't remember what it is— "I told you. I'm seeing someone. Go find someone else to occupy your free night."

With a huff and a spin, Miss Tits and Ass walks down the stairs—stomps down—keeping her head high and leaving a sickening trail of perfume as she goes.

As she steps off the final stair, Sami smiles and cocks her head to the side. "Bye-bye now."

It's polite and bitchy all at the same time and why I adore my best friend.

Once the door shuts at the bottom of the stairs, Sami says, "If you're seeing someone else tonight, I can go."

Leaning on the side of the doorjamb, I shake my head. "Get your ass up here."

Her cheeks rise as she climbs the steps. "Now who's bossy?"

Once she reaches me, I pull her inside, and just like I've done over the past three weeks, I shut the door and pin her against the wall. My chest is against hers and her nipples bead under the light fabric. "Me," I say with all the innocence I'm not feeling. My smile isn't the only part of my anatomy that grows. "You're right. I'm bossy and you like it."

Through the light fabric, her heartbeat quickens in time with mine.

"Tell me."

"Tell you what?" Sami asks.

"Tell me you like it."

"What if I don't?"

I stare into her gaze and go for broke. "What if I lift the skirt of your dress and finger your tight pussy? Will I find you like it?"

Her eyes blink, slower than normal, as her little pink tongue darts to her lip and disappears again. The way her heart thumps against mine tells me that I have her attention. "Well, Mr. Michaels, that's an interesting question. I've always found if you really want to know an answer, you should find out for yourself."

Fuck!

Lifting the skirt while simultaneously sliding my

hand under the waistband of her panties, I groan as my touch is met with her warm essence. Her hands come to my shoulders and her moans fill the apartment.

"You said talk." Her words are all breathy.

I bring my fingers to my lips and suck.

"I want you, Sami. I want to take you right now and convince you to amend our agreement again."

Her lust-filled gaze comes to mine. "Marshal."

My hands are against the wall on both sides of her face as my hardened cock presses against her stomach. "You are my best friend."

She nods. "I don't want to lose that."

"Then let's not."

"I have a terrible track record."

"Not with me," I say. "I've loved you since we were too young to know what real love was."

"I love you, too. Too much to..."

I shake my head. "No, Sami, I know you just emancipated yourself from tiny-dick and if I was as good of a friend as I should be, I'd let you enjoy your freedom, explore new options, spread your wings and all that bullshit."

She grins. "Bullshit?"

"Yes, because in the last three weeks, you've given me a taste" —I smirk— "a sweet-as-honey taste of what life could be like to spend the rest of mine with my best friend. And damn it, I want it."

Sami's forehead furrows. "What are you saying?"

Fuck. This wasn't how I had it planned, but I can't stop now.

I fall to one knee and eye the hem of her dress. As I take her hand, I look up at the woman who has always been in my corner. "Samantha Ann, I'm not a perfect man. You've seen me at my best and my worst. We've jumped off cliffs together and plunged deep into the lake. We've been there for each other when common sense would tell someone not to drive through a snowstorm or not to sleep on a tiny mattress. I cheered you on each time you thought you found your forever, but I have to be honest. I'm glad your track record sucks because if you look back, you know in your heart that through it all I was there. Through life's ups and downs you were there for me. I am shocked and awed by you. I never knew what I was missing. I love falling asleep next to you and waking up tangled in the sheets. I've loved you most of my life. I finally realized that I don't want you to explore more options, spread your wings or your legs for any other man. I don't want fake women and no-strings sex now, not since I've had what's real." I stand, wiping a tear from her cheek and bringing my nose to hers. "I want to make you mine in every way forever and always."

"Marshal..." she says, gripping my shoulders.

Keeping her pinned against the wall, I lift her chin and bring her lips to mine. My kiss isn't soft or gentle. No, it's hard, demanding, possessive, and primal. As my tongue probes beyond her sweet lips, I press myself against her.

When she glances toward the floor, my confidence begins to falter. "Sami, what is it?"

She looks back to me and her green eyes fill with tears, each drop breaking my heart.

"When I walked in and saw that woman here, I remembered *you*. I remembered who you are and who you have always been. I love you, Marshal. I always have. Our friendship works because we've always accepted each other, faults and all."

I stiffen my shoulders. "I have faults?"

"You have faults," she confirms. "And I've never had a problem with them, but I can't...not after what Jack did. Not ever. I can't be with someone who would cheat on me."

With the pad of my thumb, I wipe away a big fat tear that's rolling down her cheek. "Sami, I've never cheated on anyone. I've never been in a relationship. I've never wanted to be. Different women on different nights. Before that it was different girls...hell, that was what I wanted until I got a taste of something much sweeter." I lift one cheek to give her my lopsided grin. "And honey, it's more than that. You're real. You're a concert shirt and The Suds' cheeseburgers. You're also a sexy black dress and The Rooftop Restaurant. You're everything I never knew I wanted until I almost lost you."

"Lost me?"

"I would walk on hot coals for your smile, Sami. I know you told me not to look at you in those pictures, but I did." When she starts to look down, I lift her chin again. "Honey, you're fucking sexy, but what struck me was how sad you looked. If you'll agree to make one last amendment to our agreement, to be mine forever and always, I will work to keep your smile bright and no sadness."

"Life has sadness, Marshal."

I nod. "It does, but I'd rather focus on what makes us happy."

"What exactly are you saying?"

"I want all of you. I want" —I can barely believe the words I'm saying— "us. I want to wake up and fall asleep with you. I want to piss you off and make up. I want to taste your honey and I want you on your knees. I want us to make love all night long and when you're ready to give up your newfound freedom, I want to take it further."

With each of my statements, Sami's eyes widen.

"Further?"

I shake my head. "I don't know. This is new to me. Marriage, kids...grandkids."

Her lips come together as she swallows. "What if," she asks, "after Jack, I'm not ready?"

"Then I'll wait...as long as you let me do all the other stuff, starting today."

She shakes her head. "Marshal, are you really talking *forever and always*. You said you never wanted that."

"Blame it on my inability to see what is right in front of me. The way I look at it, who better to live the rest of my life with, to spend my forever and always with than my best friend?"

Her serious expression breaks into a smile, yet the tears continue to fall. "When?"

"Tonight, Saturday night, or in five years. Sami, it's up to you."

"You'll let me wait and not push me?"

I lean against her. "Oh, honey, I'll push you. I'll keep pushing you to try new things. I'll push you to smile and laugh. I won't push you for a date to marry you, but when you're ready, I'd like to buy you a ring, one you help pick out, and one you're willing to wear forever."

"Forever and always."

"Can we agree?"

"I agree to an engagement. I love you, Marshal. I think I always have."

"Fuck, I'm engaged."

"So am I."

"That is convenient," I say.

Sami reaches out and frames my cheeks just before she pulls my lips to hers. When we finally break away, she says, "I do, Marshal."

"Aren't you supposed to save that for the ceremony?"

She shakes her head. "I do—like it when you're bossy."

"Good, because I'm going to take off this pretty little dress and claim the one part of my best friend that will be only mine."

"Marshal?"

I kiss her again. "No arguing, honey, it was in the fine print of that agreement that you said yes to. I get all of you from this day forth."

Instead of reaching for her dress, she begins to unbutton the front of my shirt. "Only after I get to tend to your monster cock on my knees."

Oh yes. She can be bossy, too.

CHAPTER

Sami

Six months later

I can't describe the way I feel on Marshal's arm as his fiancée.

It's right.

It's easy.

It's light.

Even dressed up for a party at Marshal's boss's home, the stuffiness and pretense I hadn't realized surrounded me at events like this with the person who now and forever will be referred to as tiny-dick is gone. There is no wondering if Marshal will approve of my dress or hair or weight. The simple memory of the way Marshal looked at me when I stepped from our bedroom in this tiny black dress warms my skin and twists my core.

It's as if with only his sexy blue eyes, he can speak volumes, lavish praise, and make me feel loved and adored. I can only hope he feels the same when I look at him because I do love and adore him too.

Yes, it is *our* bedroom.

Living in two places wasn't working for us.

I'm still not ready to say the vows. It has nothing to do with my best friend, my lover, and my fiancé. It's all me and I know that. With each passing day and night, my resurrected belief in forever and always is growing.

It still amazes me that my always has been beside me forever.

And through it all, Marshal is being patient with me. There's no rush, and right now, we're enjoying all of the benefits that accompany being engaged to your best friend.

Since Marshal had time remaining on his apartment lease and the market is—for lack of a better word—fantastic, we decided to move in together into his apartment. It's not our forever home.

I happen to know a fantastic architect, and we've been discussing the finer points of our one-day dream home. Not once during our conversations has either of us mentioned median income, the best private schools, or access to the country club.

Considering that my condo sold the day it went on the market, our conversations regarding the future have a lot of luster.

"I'm so glad you both could make it," Kristy McMann says as she opens the front door and Marshal and I step inside her home, brushing the snow from our shoes. She reaches for my hand. "Oh, Sami, it is nice to finally meet you. Jason tells me that you're the best thing to happen to Marshal, and to think, the two of you have been friends most of your lives."

"Best friends."

"Since five years old," Marshal adds.

My cheeks rise into a grin, enjoying the familiarity of the man at my side. From his soft blue eyes, chiseled jaw, and broad shoulders to everything hiding under his suit, I know that I'm getting a not only handsome man but a good one. "I think we both know how unusual and special what we have is."

Kristy shakes her head with a smile as she takes our overcoats. "I just adore good love stories." She lifts her chin toward the open living room decorated for the holidays and filled with others from McMann Architectural and their companions. "Please, enjoy yourselves. There's food and drinks" —she leans close— "and I'm hoping it is all eaten, so please..."

The McManns' home is beautiful and grand; set outside Grand Rapids, it sits on over twenty-five acres placed on a hill over a lake. From the large windows, we can see out to the now-frozen lake as the moon reflects off the shimmering snow.

After talking to Marshal's boss and with drinks in hand, Marshal smiles at me as we approach a lovely woman. I know without the introduction who she is. She is Melinda Beavo, one of the key members of the team that with Marshal helped to land the big Sirius

Hotel deal and even more importantly, someone he considers a friend and mentor.

For some reason, our paths haven't crossed before now, and after all the great things Marshal has said, I'm more than excited to meet her.

Melinda turns as we come to a stop. "Oh, you're Sami."

"I am," I say. "And Melinda, I've heard so many wonderful things about you."

A confident smile brightens her expression. "I'm surprised. You see, when Marshal's not working on securing multibillion-dollar deals, your fiancé seems to have only one subject on his mind."

Sex.

With Marshal I was confident that subject would be sex.

Warmth fills my cheeks. "I hope he doesn't overshare."

"Only about how much he loves you."

"Marshal," Jason calls from near the temporary bar. "Come over here a minute. We have a debate about..."

Marshal squeezes my hand. "Will you be all right?"

"I promise to take care of her," Melinda says as I nod.

"He's a bit overprotective," I say by way of an excuse.

"So I've noticed."

"I'm capable of slaying my own dragons, but it's nice to have Marshal in my corner."

"You are." Melinda nods. "You slew a big one and I commend you for the choice you made."

The small hairs on the back of my neck stand to attention. "Excuse me?"

"I don't want to talk out of school..."

"Is this about me or Marshal?" I ask.

Melinda leads me away from the crowd to a more secluded corner near a decorated tree that must be fifteen feet high. "I hope you don't mind me mentioning your ex."

"You know my ex?"

"Unfortunately."

This makes me laugh. "I guess you do. In all honesty, he's not my favorite subject." I nod toward the windows. "Snowstorms are more interesting."

Melinda grins. "You see, Jackson has done some work for my husband—in the past." She lowers her tone. "I'm assuming that you've heard what happened?"

I shake my head. "Honestly, I haven't made it a priority to keep up on him."

One of her hands goes to her chest as her fingers flutter near her necklace. "Well, I'm not one for gossip, but considering that you told him to hit the road and Wilson et al went to extraordinary measures to keep everything under wraps, I wondered if you knew."

I shift on my tall heels. "Oh, Melinda, I'm intrigued."

"Jackson Carmichael is no longer with the legal firm of Wilson et al."

"He's not?"

"The official word is that he resigned and moved back to the Detroit area to open his own practice near his family."

My expression undoubtedly gave away my thoughts. The last thing Jackson wanted was a small private practice chasing ambulances. He had visions of greatness, wealth and fame that came with being a part of a big practice. "That doesn't sound like him."

Her lips form a straight line as she shakes her head. "My husband, Dwayne, was told in confidence that Jackson was let go."

"But he was a partner."

"Revoked."

My brow furrows. "Are you sure?" I ask.

She nods. "There was an internal incident regarding an intern."

I suck in a breath and work to keep my facial expression from screaming too much information. "Incident."

"Dwayne didn't get all of the gory details, but he seems to believe it involved possible legal repercussions. Wilson et al worked as an intermediary to satisfy both parties, not that Jackson is probably satisfied. From what I heard, the intern agreed to a settlement that along with financial compensation included Jackson Carmichael's termination from Wilson et al." Melinda shakes her head. "To accomplish that, the intern must have had some damning evidence of something significant enough that Wilson et al didn't want the association."

"Well. I should say that I'm surprised." I was surprised that Ellen would use the photos of herself. She would have had to have shown them as evidence. I suppose when she came to me and asked for them, I could have said the same thing Marshal and I did about a ride to Grand Rapids. Then again, I decided that despite Ellen's transgressions, she also was a victim of his photo fetish. Marshal and I involved her—whether intentionally or not—the day we all spoke at the bed and breakfast.

I didn't hand Ellen the photos or even the flash drive. I simply provided her with the name of the file. As Jackson's intern, she said she had access to his email. If he was stupid enough to still have the photos there, that's on him. When Jack changed his password, I only knew that the pictures of me were gone.

I'd deleted those.

The decision to take that evidence further was in Ellen's court.

From what Melinda is saying, it sounds as though she took that opportunity.

"What happened to the intern?" I ask.

Melinda shrugs. "I don't know, but if she was the injured party, I hope she received more than a settlement. I hope she received a glowing recommendation to another firm."

A smile came to my lips as a warm hand splayed long fingers over my lower back and a solid body came to my side.

"What are you two whispering about?" Marshal's deep voice asks with an edge of curiosity.

As I take a breath, Melinda looks at me and I nod. She then gives Marshal the short version of what she'd only seconds earlier shared with me.

My fiancé's mouth is agape as he looks from Melinda to me and back. "How long have you known this?"

"For a couple of weeks."

"And you didn't tell me?" Marshal asks.

Melinda looks my way and winks. "I was waiting to meet the mighty woman who was first in line at kicking Carmichael's ass to the curb."

Marshal pulls me against his side. "She is a mighty woman, and whether it's a kick or a right hook, she's a wonder. I'm thrilled to have her beside me."

"If you don't mind me asking, if the two of you aren't having a family-only small wedding, Dwayne and I would be honored to watch as two people who have always been right for one another make it official."

"We don't have any plans yet," I say, "but I'm sure that once we do, Marshal will let you know."

CHAPTER
Thirty

Sami
Six months later

"You're radiant," my mom says, her arm around my growing waist as we stand together in the long mirror. My dress is less elaborate than the one we found over a year ago. However, just like that day, her eyes are on me and mine are on her.

Mom reaches for my hand. "Samantha, you are radiant. Your dad and I are so happy about Marshal. I've never seen you happier, ever."

I lay my hand over my growing baby. "I know this was a shock. Believe it or not, I was on birth control."

Mom shakes her head. "A good shock, sweetheart. We're going to have another grandchild. How could we be upset?"

The door to the bridal room bursts open as Millie and Jane enter with Jane's two children in tow.

"Aunt Sami," her little boy Patrick says, "you look real pretty."

His sister Leigh grins. "Mommy said after you get married, you can have a baby."

I crouch down and straighten Patrick's bowtie and look at Leigh's dress. "That's right. But first, I need your help with the wedding. Are you both ready to walk down the aisle?"

They both nod.

"Just because you look amazing in an off-the-rack dress from Target doesn't mean I'm going to follow suit," Millie says as I stand and she hugs me, peering over my shoulder into the mirror.

Marshal and I had agreed we wanted a small and private wedding, nothing like the huge extravaganza I'd had planned with tiny-dick. We only wanted the people we love and those who love us. It turns out that includes half of Johnson and a significant portion of Grand Rapids.

To compromise, we found a beautiful wedding venue created from a refurbished barn.

The ceremony is to be outside, under the blue sky and the reception will be bigger than we planned. This time, Marshal and I insisted on paying for everything, well, almost.

Jane smiles at Mom as she comes to my side. "Something old." She drapes a string of pearls around my neck.

As my fingers flutter over the necklace, my mom tells the story that I already know. "These were given to your great-grandmother on her wedding day by your great-grandfather. My mother wore them in her wedding, your two aunts wore them, and so did I."

"And so did I," Jane says. "Now they're yours to hold onto until the next one of us girls is married."

We all turned to Millie.

"That would be me," she says, wiggling her engagement ring. Yes, my little sister was almost married before me.

Almost.

Her wedding is in two months, which is another reason Marshal and I didn't want my parents to pay. When it comes to Millie's wedding, I hope my bridesmaid dress will fit.

Just as I told Mom long ago, that's what alterations are for.

Even though I adore my friends, by keeping this wedding small, I only asked my sisters to stand up with me. Marshal's brother, Marcus, is his best man and my brother, Bryon, will also stand on his side.

Nothing has ever felt so right as the idea of the Michaelses and Andersons officially coming together as one big family.

There's a knock on the door.

"If that's Marshal, tell him he can't see his bride until the ceremony," Jane says.

Mom nods as she opens the door a sliver and peers out. "Monica."

Marshal's mother.

"Would you mind if I come say something to Sami?"

I nod as Mom looks my way.

"Come on in," Mom says.

I grin as Marshal's mom smiles my way.

"You're beautiful, Sami."

"Thank you."

She clutches my hands. "You have always been like a daughter to me. You know that, I hope."

I nod, swallowing the emotions that are multiplying within me faster than the hormones.

"You may already have something, but" —she opens her clutch and pulls out a sapphire-and-diamond bracelet— "George gave this to me on our wedding day. It was for my something new and something blue. I always imagined giving it to my daughter on her wedding day." She places it in my hand and closes my fingers around it. "Today, I am. It's yours, Sami. Maybe you're carrying a girl and one day it can be hers. Or maybe you'll be like me and leave it to the good Lord to knock some sense into your son and give you the perfect daughter."

I open my fingers. "Oh, Monica, I'll wear it and cherish it, but I can't keep it."

"You can, Sami. I trust you with it, just like I trust you with my son. You know that Marshal has always been my unpredictable child." She looks at Mom. "We all have at least one of those."

Mom laughs. "He's marrying mine."

Monica squeezes my hand. "And I couldn't be happier."

The seconds and minutes tick by as a photographer takes pictures and my dad appears, looking dashing in his dress pants, bow tie, and suspenders. It is Marshal's one demand—regarding the wedding, no suit coats. He wants things as casual as possible. I look down and smile at my dad's shoes. I believe that despite the fact he's lived in Michigan his entire life, he is wearing his first pair of cowboy boots.

Dad lifts his foot and tugs up the leg of his slacks. "Marshal explained how they're good for kicking zombies during the apocalypse."

"I think your supplies are now complete."

"I didn't know about the boot part. If I had, I'd have had a pair a long time ago."

I kiss his cheek.

He walks me to the doorway. The children have gone ahead with their pillow and flower petals. Millie has gone and Jane just stepped away. I place my hand in the crook of Dad's arm.

"I love you, Sami girl. Tell me that Marshal makes you happy."

"He does."

"Tell me he's good to you."

"He is."

"Tell me you love him."

"Always, Dad. Always."

My dad kisses my cheek. "Then it's time to get you hitched."

We walk together down the grass-covered aisle. As soon as we turn the corner, I see him, I see Marshal and as our eyes meet, I feel as if my heart will burst. He's the entire package. He's sexy and dirty when we're alone. He's caring and trusting. He's honest and loving. He's my protector and my cheerleader. He knows what I need before the thought crosses my mind.

He's my best friend.

My lover.

My confidant.

My companion.

He's my forever.

My always one.

EPILOGUE

Sami
A year later

"*I* can't believe we actually took Mitchell to my parents' house for the weekend so we can have sex," I say, lying back in the crook of Marshal's arm on the outdoor sofa on our back porch. Before us is a hazy sky covering the countryside.

Before Mitch was born, Marshal and I both decided to move back to Johnson. Living here makes our commutes to work longer, but it is worth the drive to have our dream home, land for our son to roam, and both sets of our parents nearby.

In a nutshell, Johnson isn't slumming it. Johnson is home and where we met.

Marshal and I want Mitch and any future children to have a childhood like we had.

Who knows, maybe when our son is five, he'll meet his always one.

"Oh," Marshal says, "he's not at Jean and Paul's just so we can have sex anywhere and everywhere without traumatizing Mitch for life." His blue eyes twinkle. "This is our anniversary and I have plans for you, Mrs. Michaels. Be prepared for a weekend of pampering."

I love everything about my husband, but if I had to choose one—one thing over his monster cock—I think it would be the way he sees me, really sees me. It's as if he sees into my soul.

I push out my bottom lip. "So no sex?"

He teases rogue strands of my hair away from my face with his long finger. "Oh, honey, there will be an excessive amount of sex."

"Okay, and now tell me more about this pampering."

"I was thinking we'll get all dressed up and head into Grand Rapids, dinner at The Rooftop and dancing at that club on the river."

I keep my expression from changing, but the truth is that after a week of work and motherhood, the last thing I want to do is get dressed up and go out.

"What do you think?" he asks with a cocky grin.

I don't want to disappoint him.

"It sounds nice," I say as I start to stand. "I'll go change." I look at his casual attire—what he changed into after work—and add. "You should shave."

"Oh." He catches my attention. "I laid something out on the bed for you to wear."

I spin around, my expression no longer hidden. "You did what?"

"I think you'll be stunning."

My lips come together as I open the glass door that leads into the kitchen. My mind is so consumed with the idea that Marshal would even consider this to be a good idea that I don't notice the shining clean countertops or the dust-free floor as I practically stomp down the hallway to our bedroom. As I push open the doors, I stop, staring at the bed.

The covers are pulled back and on my pillow is an envelope.

There isn't a dress laid out.

There's nothing but a note.

I take a quick peek over my shoulder, but the hallway is empty.

Slowly, I step closer to the bed and lift the square envelope.

On the front, in Marshall's messy handwriting, it reads: ***Happy Anniversary***.

Tears threaten the back of my eyes as I pull open the flap and ease out the piece of stationery. I unfold the piece of thick paper.

. . .

Sami,

You are my everything. I can't believe we've been married for a year or that together we made the most perfect little human or that we've managed to keep him alive and thriving. If I could wish one thing for Mitch, it would be that one day he marries his best friend.

Thank you for jumping off the cliff with me, trusting me, and loving me.

You were probably mad when I said what I said, about having something laid out for you and going out dining and dancing. (I've had this planned. I hope I was able to say it with a straight face.)

Your pampering started earlier today. The house is clean and laundry is done. If I have my way, you'll be able to rest and relax, spend your weekend on your back or knees or...we'll figure it out.

A smile comes to my lips as I imagine exactly what he means. I continue reading.

This weekend, as we celebrate our anniversary, I hope you'll spend the entire weekend wearing what is on the bed because you're definitely stunning when you wear nothing at all.

   I love you more every day,
   Your Always One

I look up to see my husband leaning against the door jamb, his blue eyes twinkling, and an oh-so-sexy grin on his lips. As I scan from his light brown hair to his handsome face, his chiseled jaw with just the right amount of beard growth to tantalize my sensitive skin, his wide chest, muscular arms, and long legs, I decide that Marshal does know me. He knows me better than anyone.

"What do you say, Mrs. Michaels?" he asks.

I drop the note and walk toward him. Laying my hand on his chest, I look up into his baby-blue eyes. "I say I love you. Did you really clean the house?"

"No, our moms did. But don't be mad. I asked them and they were happy to do something for the anniversary and give us a weekend to ourselves. Jean even invited my parents to dinner so Mitch will get plenty of attention."

"I'm not mad. Whatever will I do all weekend?"

"I believe it was laid out in that note."

"Oh," I say with a grin, "that's right."

"Do we have an agreement?"

"Under one condition."

"What would that be, Mrs. Michaels?"

I rub my palm over his bristly cheek. "Don't shave."

His smile grows. "Still so bossy." He kisses me. "I was thinking that instead of The Rooftop, we could go to The Suds for a fat cheeseburger and fries."

"I like that. But if I eat all that, I could fall asleep and according to that note, I have a weekend filled with various positions on my schedule."

"You're right, honey, you do. But you'll need sustenance to maintain that schedule and sleeping will have to wait. Because after we eat, we're coming back here and I'm having dessert. Your only job is to come, over and over and over."

Marshal's words and timbre, combined with the way he's looking at me, have my core twisted and my nipples pebbled. "How do you do that?"

"Do what?"

"Make me wet without even touching me."

"Are you wet?"

I tilt my head. "You could find out."

"Shit," he says, as he lifts the blouse I wore to work over my head and lavishes his attention on my breasts. "Our reservations at The Suds can wait."

"Always."

Thank you for reading My Always One

If you enjoyed this lighter side of Aleatha, be sure to check out her other "lighter" ones: **PLUS ONE, ONE NIGHT, A SECRET ONE,** *and* **ANOTHER ONE.** *You can get each one individually, or grab all three in the box set,* **ALL ONES.**

If more mystery and danger is your cup of tea, be sure to check out Aleatha's latest enemies-to-lovers, age-gap, arranged-marriage duet, The Devil's Series Duet – FATES DEMAND *(free prequel),* **DEVIL'S DEAL,** *and* **ANGEL'S PROMISE.**

Coming soon is Aleatha's new dangerous romance series THE SIN SERIES, *starting with* WHITE RIBBON *(prequel) and* **RED SIN** *(book one).*

WHAT TO DO NOW

LEND IT: Did you enjoy MY ALWAYS ONE? Do you have a friend who'd enjoy MY ALWAYS ONE? MY ALWAYS ONE may be lent one time. Sharing is caring!

RECOMMEND IT: Do you have multiple friends who'd enjoy my dark romance with twists and turns and an all new sexy and infuriating anti-hero? Tell them about it! Call, text, post, tweet...your recommendation is the nicest gift you can give to an author!

REVIEW IT: Tell the world. Please go to the retailer where you purchased this book, as well as Goodreads, and write a review. Please share your thoughts about MY ALWAYS ONE on:

*Amazon, MY ALWAYS ONE Customer Reviews

*Barnes & Noble, MY ALWAYS ONE, Customer Reviews

*iBooks, MY ALWAYS ONE Customer Reviews

* BookBub, MY ALWAYS ONE Customer Reviews

*Goodreads.com/Aleatha Romig

WEB OF SIN:

SECRETS

October 2018

LIES

December 2018

PROMISES

January 2019

TANGLED WEB:

TWISTED

May 2019

OBSESSED

July 2019

BOUND

August 2019

WEB OF DESIRE:

SPARK

Jan. 14, 2020

FLAME

February 25, 2020

ASHES

April 7, 2020

DANGEROUS WEB:

Prequel: "Danger's First Kiss"

DUSK

November 2020

DARK

January 2021

DAWN

February 2021

$$* \; * \; *$$

THE INFIDELITY SERIES:

BETRAYAL

Book #1

October 2015

CUNNING

Book #2

January 2016

DECEPTION

Book #3

May 2016

ENTRAPMENT

Book #4

September 2016

FIDELITY

Book #5

January 2017

* * *

THE CONSEQUENCES SERIES:

CONSEQUENCES

(Book #1)

August 2011

TRUTH

(Book #2)

October 2012

CONVICTED

(Book #3)

October 2013

REVEALED

(Book #4)

Previously titled: Behind His Eyes Convicted: The Missing Years

June 2014

BEYOND THE CONSEQUENCES

(Book #5)

January 2015

RIPPLES (Consequences stand-alone)

October 2017

CONSEQUENCES COMPANION READS:

BEHIND HIS EYES-CONSEQUENCES

January 2014

BEHIND HIS EYES-TRUTH

March 2014

* * *

STAND ALONE MAFIA THRILLER:

PRICE OF HONOR

Available Now

* * *

THE LIGHT DUET:

Published through Thomas and Mercer Amazon exclusive

INTO THE LIGHT

June 2016

AWAY FROM THE DARK

October 2016

* * *

TALES FROM THE DARK SIDE SERIES:

INSIDIOUS

(All books in this series are stand-alone erotic thrillers)

Released October 2014

* * *

ALEATHA'S LIGHTER ONES:

PLUS ONE

Stand-alone fun, sexy romance

May 2017

ANOTHER ONE

Stand-alone fun, sexy romance

May 2018

ONE NIGHT

Stand-alone, sexy contemporary romance

September 2017

A SECRET ONE

April 2018

* * *

INDULGENCE SERIES:

UNEXPECTED

August 2018

UNCONVENTIONAL

January 2018

UNFORGETTABLE

October 2019

UNDENIABLE

August 2020

ABOUT THE AUTHOR

Aleatha Romig is a New York Times, Wall Street Journal, and USA Today bestselling author who lives in Indiana, USA. She has raised three children with her high school sweetheart and husband of over thirty years. Before she became a full-time author, she worked days as a dental hygienist and spent her nights writing. Now, when she's not imagining mind-blowing twists and turns, she likes to spend her time with her family and friends. Her other pastimes include reading and creating heroes/anti-heroes who haunt your dreams!

Aleatha impresses with her versatility in writing. She released her first novel, CONSEQUENCES, in August of 2011. CONSEQUENCES, a dark romance, became a bestselling series with five novels and two companions released from 2011 through 2015. The compelling and epic story of Anthony and Claire Rawlings has graced more than half a million e-readers. Her first stand-alone smart, sexy thriller INSIDIOUS was next. Then Aleatha released the five-novel INFIDELITY series, a romantic suspense saga, that took the reading world by storm, the final book landing on three of the top bestseller lists. She ventured into traditional publishing with Thomas and Mercer. Her books INTO THE LIGHT and AWAY FROM THE DARK were published through this mystery/thriller publisher in 2016. In the spring of 2017, Aleatha again ventured into a different genre with her first fun and sexy stand-alone romantic comedy with the USA Today bestseller PLUS ONE. She continued with ONE NIGHT and ANOTHER ONE. If you like fun, sexy, novellas that make your heart pound, try her INDULGENCE SERIES. In 2018 Aleatha returned to her dark romance roots with SPARROW WEBS.

Aleatha is a "Published Author's Network" member of the Romance Writers of America and PEN America. She is represented by Kevan Lyon of Marsal Lyon Literary Agency and Dani Sanchez with Wildfire Marketing.

facebook.com/aleatharomig
twitter.com/aleatharomig
instagram.com/aleatharomig